LOVING IN MY WORLD IS NEVER EASY

THE STREETS
& THE PULPIT

LOVING IN MY WORLD IS NEVER EASY

THE STREETS & THE PULPIT

TATIANA

ISBN: 9798341428331

Cover design by Tatiana Timmons

Printed in the United States of America

Synopsis

As the Zoo Boyz brotherhood teeters on the brink of collapse, the story unfolds further as Preach grapples with the ultimate choice of siding with the streets or the pulpit. Between trying to be the perfect Preacher's kid and remaining a friend to his brothers, his faith never wavers. During the Zoo Boyz's quest to understand Chevy's inexplicable desire to travel, Preach crossed paths with an individual who would alter the course of his life in ways he never imagined. Navi enters Preach's heart like a thief in the night. She struggles to choose between her career and the man she believes is meant for her.

As Preach and Navi take on each other, Chevy is determined to embark on his trip, but the obstacles he encounters throw a ranch in his plans when he comes across Bookstore Girl. With no intention of seeking the affection of a female companion, Chevy becomes captivated by Bookstore Girl, adding saving her to his checklist.

Everyone is straddling the fence, but which side will they choose?

"Every woman wants the perfect man, even if she falls in love with him in a book."

- Tatiana

Trigga Warnings

"I think we need to warn them, Chev."

Preach.

"Man, fuck all that they wanted to hear your story so let's tell them."

Chevy.

"I think we should pray first."

Preach.

"Preach, nigga don't start with all that. If you want to warn they ass, then do it nigga. I don't have time to waste."

Chevy.

"Says the mystery man. All you niggas want to do is be in charge. Let me tell them then."

Bookstore Girl/Zaria.

"Wait, Zaria this isn't your story to tell, it's Preach story."

Navi.

"Of course you're going to have his back you're fucking him."

Bookstore Girl/Zaria.

"Cut the fucking semantics get to the point or I'm out!"

Chevy.

"Fuck it, fine. Before reading this just say a small prayer. We always want to give God the glory. However, we CUSS, we FUCK, we KILL, we don't GIVE A FUCK about NOTHING or NO ONE. We're all HOOD, but I'm a little HOLY. We all have TRAUMA, but most of all we PRAY!"

Preach.

"Yeah, and if you not with none of it then exit the kindle or close the fucking book. The rest of y'all come see what we're talking about. Fuck with us one time and make sure you talk to a nigga nice because none of us are perfect!"

Chevy.

Tati Thoughts

Whew! The abundance of love I received for the Zoo Boyz was truly unexpected. Y'all showed out for me, and I want to show out for you all. Thank You so much!

If this is your first time here. I highly recommend reading Zoo Boyz before diving into this book!

Now, first, the font! I heard everybody; I did. However, the orange makes my book authentic and me removing the color just doesn't feel right. My boys want the orange, it makes them standout. So, I found a compromise and I hope you all enjoy and understand. If not, then maybe visiting the Zoo is just not for you and that's ok.

As we continue with the story, we're picking up where we left off. We're going into Preach's perspective and slowing it down a bit. Please keep in mind that each guy has their own personality, meaning the spice level of each book will be different. Some books may have way more than others, but don't get Preach twisted because he definitely gets down. Now let's get to the fun shit and remember.

We Only Fuck With The Zoo!

Table of Content

Playlist

Y'all know we vibe and read over here. Please know you can add the playlist via apple music by following: Freshiebabii

The Remorse- Drake - Prologue
Imported Couches- Larry June Pg. 9-16
Conversation- Dawn Richard Pg.40-44
Nasty- Jousha Showtime Williams Pg.51-54
It's Over Now- Deborah Cox Pg.59-61
Turn Yo Clic Up (mixed)– Future & Quavo Pg.64-71
Precious Moments- Portrait Pg.88-93
Blessings- Big Sean Ft. Drake Pg.94-99
You Send Me- Sam Cooke Pg.104-105
Angel In Disguise- Brandy Pg.106-109
The Rain - K. Michelle Pg.114-118
Wild Side- Normani ft. Cardi B Pg.133-136
Came to Party- Future & Metro Boomin Pg.137-140
Tadow- Masego & FKJ Pg.141-145
Life's A B*tch- Nas Pg.163-166
Saturn- SZA Pg.167-169
Discipline- Janet Jackson Pg.170-176
Tell Him The Truth- Keri Hilson Pg.177-179

Deliver Me (This Is My Exodus)- Donald Lawrence & The Tri-City Singers ft Le'Andria Johnson Pg.186-191

The Color Orange

Optimism, happiness, enthusiasm, and Connections. As well as displaying creativity, positivity, Transformation, and enlightenment. The color can make people feel outgoing or Bold, and can Strengthen The Emotional Body, encouraging joy, well-being, and cheerfulness. Orange can also project feelings of arrogance, Pride, impatience, superficiality, and Lack of Seriousness.

PROLOGUE

PRENTICE
BEFORE ZOO

"I told you, Prentice, if you cannot follow my rules and the word of God, you cannot be in my home," my father said to me as I stood outside his front door.

"I have nowhere to go. I've been down bad pops. I'm your son," I pleaded.

My father put me out a few years back. At first, things were okay; I had a job that provided less than the minimum. Diamond had come around when I needed a friend the most. I was in a vulnerable state, and he removed me from that space. I had been staying in hotels, then moved in with Diamond's grandma. I'd met him in church. He was cool; he understood where I was coming from. However, I couldn't live with Grandma G permanently.

For my father, I had hit my third strike, and he just wouldn't let me live it down. My senior year of high school, I'd got caught fucking a cheerleader in the bathroom. The Christian academy I went to had a tolerance for nothing, so they kicked me out. It disappointed him, but for me, it was a moment of freedom. Then, he sent me off to ministry school. Although I could have completed it, I dropped out. I felt forced into something I wasn't ready for. The final straw for him was when he'd caught me smoking in his home. It was either his way or no way.

Being a preacher's kid was something nobody understood. It's similar to being the kid of a celebrity or someone with a high social status. Many people view preacher kids as being perfect. To hold the name of our parents or follow behind them. I was none of that. Yeah, I loved coming to church praising God in times of worship, but trapped between being on the pulpit alongside my father and in the streets was a battle. My father prided himself on following the word.

I needed his help, and he was completely turning his back on me. Not only did I disappoint him, but so did my mother. She was an addict. He didn't believe in divorce, but after trying to save her so many times, he had given up and did what he felt was right. However, through the years, he kept his head high and kept it moving.

He went to close the door, but I stopped him. "You say you're a man of God. You're supposed to forgive; what happened to that?"

He snatched the door out of my hand. "Prentice, I'm holy, but my hands are not, so you watch it, boy. I forgive you. I pray for you every day, but you cannot stay here," he said as he closed the door in my face.

I dropped my head. I had nothing, not even my mother. I walked through the streets, trying to decide if I was going to go back to Grandma G's or thug it out by myself. I texted Diamond to meet up with me. I'd been walking for about thirty minutes when I glanced across the street to see someone that caught my attention. I jogged across, following behind her. She staggered as she walked further up the street into the nearest alley. She walked behind the big dumpster. I went to peek but heard her pissing, so I backed away. Then I heard nothing. I peeked only to see her tying an elastic band around her arm.

Seeing her like this pissed me off. I closed my eyes, saying a prayer, the same prayer I've been repeating since I was thirteen. God wasn't listening, though, because it was still going on. "Ma!" I shouted.

Her eyes raised to me in shock. "Pr-Prentice," she mumbled.

I dropped my head because every time I saw her this way, it broke my heart. How was it a woman who was bright, beautiful, healthy, and a woman of God like this? He was to take care of his kids, no? I felt like both my parents had turned their backs on me. This isn't what I prayed for. She had now focused back on what she was doing as if I weren't standing in front of her. She tapped her arm a few times as she blew out a heavy breath in frustration. "Prentice," she whined.

I leaned forward, trying to help her up, but she grabbed my hands. Her eyes met mine, and I knew it was coming. The horror of how she fucked me up when I was young flashed in my head. From helping her shoot up at a young age to watching niggas take advantage of her in front of my eyes. When my father found out, he took me away from her, but somehow, I always ran back. If God were a forgiving one, why couldn't I be?

"I just need something to make me sleep is all. After this, I promise I'm done. I'm going to come to church, and we can be like we were before," she said.

My mother had lost her damn mind. I wasn't thirteen anymore. I'm twenty-six. I was a far cry from the child I used to be. "You got to quit this shit, it's killing you," I gritted.

My phone vibrated in my pocket, and I knew it was Diamond, but this was more important. It was my mother, the person I'd loved with my soul. I snatched the syringe out of her hand. Her eyes widened, and she began attacking me. Her arms swung wildly as she tried to get the syringe from me.

"Get off me!" I shouted.

She was like a wild animal in rage. I shoved her off me. "Fuck is wrong with you? You gone beat my ass over this?"

I threw it on the ground and stomped on it before walking off. I bumped into someone who was walking with two other niggas. I didn't pay them any attention until I heard my mother's screams. I turned to go back and help her. Yes, I was mad, but I wasn't about to let another nigga abuse her. I rushed back over, snatching the nigga that was on her by his shirt.

Whap! Whap!

"Fuck is you doing nigga!"

He and I tussled in the alley. "The bitch owes me money!" he yelled.

"Prentice, puh-lease, it's okay," I heard her whine.

I didn't care. I was protecting her. I continued to pound on him as his boys tried getting me off.

Whap! Whap!

Fist to his body. Fist to his face. He had finally pushed me off him.

Click, Click!

"We ain't doing that, my boy," one guy held a gun to my back.

I let the guy go, throwing up my hands.

Bloaw! Bloaw!

The sound of the gunshots made me jump. That's when Diamond stepped on one side of me while another nigga, who I didn't know, came up on the other side. They both held guns out to the guy I was fighting with. "How much she owes you?" the guy I didn't know asked.

While the two men lay on the ground, one screaming in agony, the other looking to the heavens, dead. Their partner stood there with a smirk. "More than you niggas can afford." He laughed.

"I asked a question. Now you can answer and get your bread, or I can just put one in yo head. Nobody out here checking for a low-budget ass dealer."

He began laughing like he didn't have a gun pointed at him. My mom stepped in the way, and he shoved her. I snatched the gun from the guy's hand, moving closer, pressing the barrel into his chest. I was angry not just with this situation, but of my own. "Nigga he asked you a question, and you ain't answer. You might want to start praying, now."

My mom came to the side of me. "Don't do—"

Bloaw!

The bullet entered his chest, exiting his back. I inhaled deeply, then turned and threw up. I'd never killed anyone before. This was something I knew I couldn't take back. I could hear my mother screaming at the top of her lungs. I lifted, turning to her. "Shut up! This shit happened because of you. You need to get help; if you don't, you will be just like him dead!" I shouted.

Diamond came up to me, taking the gun out of my hand. "Let's go," he whispered.

As we walked off, I heard one last gunshot. Diamond's friend killed the last guy, leaving my mother standing there with the bodies. I wasn't worried about her telling the cops because, by the time she doped herself, she wouldn't remember.

"Heavenly Father, I pray they found peace before they took their last breath, Amen," I said as I continued to the car.

I didn't know how God was going to forgive me for this. I just prayed that he would. My mind had drifted off into its own world when we pulled up to a place called Orange Village. When I got out, I followed behind Diamond. As soon as I stepped inside, there were two other guys in there. Diamond pointed. "That's Zu and Foe. Y'all, this is Prentice, the one I was telling you about," he said.

"Sup," they said in unison.

"Don't you ever pull a gun out my hand again," the guy that came with Diamond said.

He walked around the room like a fucking king. "You shoot a nigga only if you must not because your emotions are getting the best of you. Your momma is a dope fiend. He won't be the last nigga that tries to beat her ass. I know you're down right now; I've been there. I want to help you," he said.

"You know we just committed a horrible sin, right?" I asked.

Zu stood, "Oh hell nah, he's too churchy for the Zoo!" he yelled.

"God is faithful; we're just not faithful to him." I paused. "You look like you can use some church!" I snapped.

I looked at Diamond, who was smiling like what happened in the alley was a fucking joke. I'd just committed the ultimate sin, something in my eyes that was unforgivable. "That's Chevy," he pointed. "I told him about you and your situation. He wanted to meet you."

I nodded. Chevy walked up to me, tossing me a bag. I opened the bag to stacks full of money. "Fifty thousand, get your shit in order. You don't have to pay me back, but I do want you to ride with us."

"I only ride for fun with Diamond's bike."

Diamond handed me a helmet and jacket that had Preach on the back. "You have one now. *Preach.* We're brothers here with Zoo. We got your back, and that's word."

Although it wasn't what I had pictured things to be like, they had looked out. Hell, Chevy saved me tonight. It could have been me lying in that alley trying to save my mother, who would have walked over my body like I didn't exist just to get high. I was vulnerable, and he protected me. I owed him my life. So, if riding bikes is what he wanted in return, then so be it. I wasn't sure if this brotherhood was as genuine as Diamond claimed, but I decided to give it a chance.

As soon as I slid the jacket on. I heard them in unison.

"Welcome to the muhfuckin Zoo!"

So much shit had went down in the last couple of weeks that I was going to need another baptism to help me through it. The more I told myself I wouldn't backslide, the more I was sliding further back. Trying to balance between my father's expectations and my current desires had become a daily battle. We had just won the race with Dragon Heat, and everyone was excited, screaming and cheering except Chevy and Zu.

I saw Chevy getting ready to ride out, but before he could, I jogged over to him. Before putting his helmet on, he saw me, "What's good Preach?"

I knew he was going through something, and it didn't help that we had fucked up, especially Zu. I knew that no matter how much each of us had asked, he wouldn't tell us nothing further than what he had already done. So, I wanted to try a different approach. "I want you to come to church Sunday. Before you say no, give it a chance, allow God to hear you. See what he says first before you make any sudden decisions."

The way he cut his eyes at me; I could tell he wanted to say something smart. "I know my nigga, but trust me. I haven't asked you for anything ever, even the night you saved my life. Think about it," I told him.

He nodded as he slid his helmet on and sped off. I headed back toward the crowd so we could take off together to the Orange Village, our hall, where we held all of our after-parties. I spotted Simone standing off in the distance, watching me, looking simple as hell. She needed to be off somewhere healing instead of out here in these streets. I liked her, but considering I knew little about her, to do what I did was enough. I saved her, and that was as much as I could do.

We all hopped on our bikes, but Zu he was fucked up; although we won, his relationship with Chevy was gone to shit, and knowing him, he fucked over Harvey too.

"Zu, nigga come on!" Diamond yelled.

Reluctantly, he hopped on his bike, and we sped off. "Aye Zu, you good my nigga?" Diamond asked as we lane switched.

"I'm straight."

"The lies you tell. You fucked up, all you got to do is fix it," Foe jumped in.

We'd stopped at a red light. Zu turned, looking at us, "Fuck you, Foe!"

I could hear Diamond laughing. "Ask Preach for some prayer."

"I done told y'all nigga's stop playing with God."

They were all being funny, but Zu already knew he messed up, and the shit was eating away at him. He didn't need us harping on it. Zu meant well; he just needed to make better decisions and get his life in order. He needed more God and less fuckery. When the light turned green, we all kept straight while Zu went left. "Where that nigga going?" I asked.

"Probably following the pussy. That nigga hooked on Harvey. She got that nigga stuck," Diamond chuckled.

Within a couple minutes, we'd made it to the Orange Village. The parking lot was packed. It was crazy to see how the city had come out to celebrate with us. We revved our bikes so people could move out of the way as we came through. When we reached the front, the first thing we heard were people chanting. "*We only fuck with the Zoo!*"

Diamond, Foe, and I glanced around. "Who the fuck are all these people?" Diamond leaned over, asking me.

"Shit, I don't know, but the first demon steps up to me; I'm sending they ass down to hell's den."

Diamond waved me off. I was serious as hell. One thing I could do was see a demon from a mile away. I got off my bike and headed into the building behind the guys.

"Aye, church boy!" a female's voice shouted.

I knew she was talking about me because none of these niggas were saved. I turned to see who it was, and it was someone I'd never seen before. She was a thick, brown thing. I was a sucker for a thick girl. Although she was attractive, I turned away from her entering the building. I had one Jezabel who tried playing with me. I wasn't letting another one do the same thing.

I couldn't believe it. It was a full house. There was barely walking space. My eyes bounced all over the crowd. Foe had just walked up to me, and before he even uttered a word, his eyes drifted off to someone walking in the building. That's when I realized he was watching her. I'd never seen this nigga so fixated on someone the way he was in this moment. *Did this nigga like Harvey?* I knew if I asked, he would deny it, so I held off.

Diamond stood on the couch in the corner holding two champagne bottles, shaking them, allowing them to spray all over the crowd. *"We don't fuck with you; we only fuck with the Zoo!"* everyone screamed.

I smiled at the abundance of love we were getting; my eyes scanned the crowd until I saw something that caught my attention. I tapped Foe, letting him know I was stepping away for a second.

"The Devil is a lie."

In and out. I coached myself.

When I called out to Preach, and he glanced at me, it was damn near breathtaking. This man was fine as hell. With a towering height and slender build, a complexion that boasted a light brown hue, and lips that seemed irresistible for a kiss. The glasses he wore just made him top-tier. However, when he blew me off, I knew approaching him wouldn't be easy, so I would have to make him come to me.

Upon entering the building, I thought the outside was crowded; it was nothing compared to the inside. I squeezed my way through the crowd, going straight to the bar. I knew I would need something strong to get me through the night. I turned to the bartender. "A double shot of cognac please."

THE STREETS & THE PULPIT

My eyes bounced all around, looking for him, but he was nowhere in sight. A pretty woman walked up to the bar, looking like her night was going to shit. "Can I get a shot, please, anything you have!"

"Long night?" I leaned in, asking.

She sighed loudly. "Yes."

"Men problems?" I asked.

The stare she gave me told me I was right. I'd wondered if it had to do with any of the Zoo Boyz. "Well, he isn't worth the stress, girl," I said, tapping her arm.

Her eyes landed on my hand as I eased it away. "Shitting me. You don't know the Zoo Boyz like I do."

The bartender handed us our drinks at the same time. I raised my glass to her as she guzzled hers down. "Fuck the Zoo Boyz," she mumbled.

I wanted to pry some more, but I chose otherwise as I walked off looking for Preach. I observed the room, and I could not spot him.

"Looking for me?" I heard a soft but deep voice ask in my ear.

A smile eased on my face as I turned toward him. "Maybe."

He bit into his bottom lip as he slowly nodded his head. He slightly leaned in. "Follow me."

Preach took me by the hand, leading me through the crowd toward the back of the building and out of the back door. I swear if I had the guts, I would fuck this man right here and right now. Once we stepped outside, he closed the door behind us, ceasing the loud music coming from inside. He gazed at me and his eyes went from soft to demonic.

"Why the fuck you in there playing Dora the Explorer looking for me?" he snapped.

I was surprised and unsure of what to say. "I-I—"

"You-you what? I don't have time for the Grandma Susie shit. I saw you in there playing hide and seek," he gritted.

I'd heard so much about this man, but the things I'd heard versus what I was seeing didn't add up. Preach leaned forward, placing his forehead to mine. I saw the chain dangle from his neck with a cross on it, so I knew his name wasn't in vain. This man smelled so good I closed my eyes, inhaling deeply.

"I'm up here," I heard him say.

Eyes on him. "Listen, I'm going to spare the rod tonight. But if I catch you around here again, yeah, well," he said, lifting his head, taking his finger, gently tapping the tip of my nose and winking. He walked back to the door, "Get yo ass on somewhere; better find Jesus, baby, 'cause Preach isn't the one," he finished, slamming the door in my face as he went back inside.

I stood there, appalled. I didn't know if it turned me on by what he did or made me upset. What I did know was Preach hadn't seen the last of me.

Ten-plus years with Zu and the nigga fucked up our friendship over dumbass choices. I could have easily forgiven him, but this wasn't the first time. It was as if the nigga's head was hollow, and he couldn't use good judgment. Then, the crew, they all somehow disappointed me by letting women come in and stir the pot. Shit was just beyond me. I sacrificed a lot for each one of them, and the thanks I get was my shit being stolen and getting locked up.

I thought about Preach's offer of me going to church. How was God going to save a nigga like me? Hell, Zoo had done some unforgivable things. I'm not sure where Preach got all this optimism from, but he was buggin'. I'd pulled up to my crib, parking my bike next to my Chevy. I had mixed feelings of excitement and apprehension about the trip. It was the fear of the unknown. I had so many questions for my mother. The main one is why? Why did she give me up, purposely placing me in the Devil's hand?

I wondered if she had other kids she'd given up. I didn't know if I hated her or what. I just wanted to meet her. I found out that my father had died a couple of years ago. Being the nigga who didn't know his parents was torture. I remember every day I would see people walk by me who, in my mind, resembled me thinking is that my mother or my father. There was a void I needed to fill, and I felt like this trip was it.

Harvey was acting scared like she didn't want to go. That alone spoke volumes because, if she were really my friend, why wouldn't she? We'd talked about it so many times. It didn't matter because, with or without her, I was leaving. I had to. I was on a mission, and this was one thing on my checklist.

As I made my way to my door, the sound of my bushes moving had me pulling my gun out and aiming it.

"Don't shoot, please," I heard Lola's voice.

I dropped my head and my gun. Lola was a bad little shorty but, too quick to fuck. She had been trying since the night I first met her. Baby girl was very needy. She came from between the bushes, scooting her feet close to me. "I wanted to surprise you after the race," she smiled.

"I appreciate you," I replied as I unlocked the door to go in.

She stood there blinking, waiting for me to tell her she could come in. I opened the door wide, giving her the signal to enter. She giggled while swaying her way into my crib.

She pulled a bottle of champagne out of her big purse. "I thought we could celebrate."

"Pop that muhfucka then."

Lola wasn't a bad person. I was just a man that went with the vibe and connection. I wanted my girl to fuck me mentally, then physically. Lola didn't have that, but she was good company for now. She popped open the bottle, making her way to my kitchen like it was hers. I grabbed my jar of weed and pulled my jacket and shirt off while she poured us up. I sat on my plush imported couch that I had gotten only two weeks ago. I grabbed the remote from the table, pressing a button which allowed the curtains to ease open, exposing the city view.

"That's so beautiful. You really have a lovely place, Chevy," I heard her coming into the living room.

"Thanks."

She handed me the glass, took her shoes off, and sat next to me, putting her fucking feet on my white couch. "Nah, sweetheart, feet on the floor," I side-eyed her.

Strike one.

She looked at me in confusion, "Oh, you're about to smoke, but I thought—"

Side eye. Strike two.

"Lola, if you don't like what I do in my shit. The door is right there, sweetheart," I told her as I licked the Rello, sealing my blunt.

She shifted her body, placing her feet on the floor. I lit my blunt, placing it to my lips as I leaned back on the couch. I had so much shit going on in my head it was hard to focus on her. Honestly, I would rather be by myself in this moment, but I was trying to be a gentleman. I must have been so focused on my weed because, by the time I turned to look at Lola, she was standing before me, naked.

The smoke lingered before, exposing her perfectly shaped body. "I want you to fuck me," she purred as she placed her hands on her wide hips.

I leaned forward, placing my elbows to my knees. I brought the blunt back up to my lips, sucking in deep, holding the smoke in my lungs. I cocked my head to the side just slightly. "Lola, you know why I won't fuck you?"

Exhale.

"Why?"

"Because you are too eager, sweetheart. If I gave you this dick, you wouldn't know how to act," I said as I stood.

I placed the blunt back to my lips. *Inhale, then exhale.* I began circling her. My fingertips tapping her collarbone. "This dick is priceless."

"I can afford it," she shot back.

I placed the blunt back to my lips. *Inhale, then exhale.*

My hand slowly caressed the side of her neck, making its way to the front gripping it, not too tight to choke her, but just enough to allow her to breathe.

"This dick is treacherous."

I placed the blunt back to my lips. *Inhale, then exhale.*

"This dick can hurt feelings."

She sucked in air. "I can take my feelings out of it."

Inhale, then exhale.

"This dick is greedy."

Her eyes closed; it turned her on. "I can be selfish," she muttered.

"This dick doesn't just fuck, it makes love."

Inhale, then exhale.

"This dick chooses who it wants to fuck," I paused, now placing my lips so close to hers I felt her hot breath. "This dick is vegan, which means it's one hundred percent organic, sweetheart. It's the purest shit you can ever imagine. Last, I'm simply not interested."

I released her neck and stepped back. Lola damn near fell forward. When she caught herself, she covered her body with her hands.

"Don't be ashamed. I'm an honest man. It's just me and you here, so relax. Let me help you put your clothes on."

Lola snatched up her dress and slid it back on. "Why are you like this? So reserved, so mean?"

I wasn't mean; I just picked who I invited in and who I shared my feelings with. When you grew up like I did, you had no choice; otherwise, people would run over you. It happened so many times in my life that I had no choice but to put up a wall, one in which I refused to let down. Especially for her.

The sound of someone coming into my house caught my attention. I knew it could only be one person because niggas weren't crazy enough to run up in my shit. When she stepped into the living room, I could tell that she had been crying.

"Harve!" Lola squealed.

"I'm going to kill him," I blurted out.

Harvey stepped forward. "No, you don't have to do all that. I'll just take the guest bedroom," she mumbled.

I glanced over at Lola. "My friend needs me. You can stay, or you can go, but Harvey comes first."

I walked over to Harvey. "Follow me."

Harvey, being in this state scared me. She had a past when things would happen to her. She didn't know how to handle it. It's why I didn't want her fucking with Zu. She needed a nigga that would cater to her feelings. One that could spot it from a mile away. Having a childhood like we did; we needed a different type of love. We needed more than just sex. We were broken. We needed people that could help put us back together.

Zu couldn't give Harvey that, but I knew Foe could. She thinks I don't know, but I saw how they looked at each other. It wasn't my place to tell her who she needed to be with. She had stepped into the Zoo, and now her life was about to flip upside down. It was the reason for me keeping her away from them for so long. Now, both worlds have come together. I was just waiting for them to collide.

When we got to my man cave, I sat on the couch, patting the side so she could sit. "What happened? Before you get to lying, don't," I told her.

She dropped her head and then brought it up slow. "Nothing really, I tried getting his attention, but he was so focused on you I felt forgotten about."

This was the start. "Yeah, well, that's Zu. Listen, with him, he's not like them other lame-ass niggas you dealt with. Zu is a different breed. He means well, but because his life is not in order, neither is he. You need a nigga with a little more structure. What about Foe?"

Her eyes widened. I watched how nervous she became. He made her feel something. I knew Harvey. She knew which way was right, but she always chose the opposite. I wasn't going to pressure her. She made it clear it was her choice, but I knew what was best.

"What about him?"

"Nothing, just know I'm watching."

She tapped my shoulder. "This trip, when are you leaving?"

I ran my hand over my head. "In a week."

"A week!"

"Yes, and I really hope you decide to come."

"Have you talked to your mother?" she asked.

I had just recently found out who she was and where she lived. I thought about it so many times, but every time I got ready to dial her number, I erased it. "No, I kind of want it to be a surprise."

"What if it's not what you expect?"

I stood from the couch. "Then it's a risk I'm willing to take."

She reached out for my hand. "Call her. I don't want to see you get hurt, Chev. Why don't you hold off just a little longer, please. I'll come with you."

I knew she was trying to stall because of Zu. It was something else I wanted to talk to her about that I had been meaning to, but she had enough for tonight, so I opted out of telling her. Before leaving the room, I stopped. "I do have something I need to take care of before taking off. I'll give you two months, Harvey. Two is all you get, and I'm off." I paused. "I don't want to see you get hurt either. But these two months are for you, not Zu," I said as I disappeared into the hall.

Maybe I needed the two months more than she did because what I had to tell her was going to break her heart for real. I knew I needed to prepare for the storm.

"No one can serve two masters. Matthew; six twenty-four through twenty-six. Do I need to remind you?" My father said as soon as I stepped into the church.

I stopped looking at him. It was early the next morning, and I was here to help him, but he wanted to preach at me. I really wasn't in the mood, but I sucked it up because, at the end of it all, I was here for God, not him. "Second Corinthians five verse seven for we walk by faith, not by sight."

He paused. "So, you do still remember your scriptures."

"Of course. You never let me forget."

He came closer to me, placing his hand on my shoulder. "Then why are you still out there? What are in those streets that's more important than being here? Are you out there getting in trouble?"

This is the part nobody has seen or experienced. Being preached to daily. He acted as if I didn't sit in the church with him on Sundays for hours. Or helped when we had church events. Bible study, I was here. I was available for God.

Nevertheless, being obliged to do something was not the answer. When I was younger, I didn't have outside friends, just the other kids that were within the church and they were just like me. Tired of everything holy.

The streets saved me; well, Chevy did. My father didn't know the type of things I'd been through since putting me out. I found a home, a place that welcomed and embraced me. I had solid niggas that had my back through dark times. Chevy came in acting as not only my brother, but a father figure, and I still made my way to this sanctuary every day. I wanted to make my father proud. I wanted him to brag about his only son, but I also wanted to experience life the way I wanted to.

He had now stepped away from me, walking over to the pulpit. He stood behind the small podium. "It took me years to get this church. I prayed daily for it. I worked two jobs just to get it. Even when the Devil came in swooping my family in his grasp." He swung his arms, mocking a hug.

I knew the Devil part was about my mother. He never really talked about it, and neither did I. He brought his hands together in a clap, ensuring that he had my complete attention. "Last night, God came to me. Spirit said a storm is coming."

He raised both hands, closed his eyes, and shook his head from side to side. He then looked at me. "Prentice, I want you to give a sermon. It's your calling, son."

"I can't do that."

"You can and you will. This young generation needs to hear from someone they can relate to. Besides, when I'm gone, it will be you standing here, not me," he said.

How did he know this is what I wanted for my future? I was a sinner, one who was trying to find his way. God hadn't called on me yet. He was trying to force me.

"I'm not ready."

"Neither was I. You're going to preach. Let God use you, son." He finished as he walked into the back.

This was the pressure of being a preacher's kid. How was I going to preach to people when I had committed more sins than the Devil himself? I didn't know what I was going to do, but I knew my father was counting on me, and what I didn't want to do was disappoint him. If he found out what I was really into out in those streets, he would never talk to me again.

"Lord, God, please see me through."

THE STREETS & THE PULPIT

I finished what I needed to do at the church and headed out.
I needed to meet up with the guys. I was about to go from
being saved to being a sinner in a matter of minutes.

ZARIA

I was on my way to my parent's house for our regular family dinner. It's what my mother called Soul Food Saturday. I had missed the last few Saturdays because I'd had so much going on, so I knew my showing up today would not go smoothly. My mother was going to have questions as she always did. I pulled into the driveway and spotted both my sisters' cars. Navanna and Rayana. My father wanted a boy but got three girls. I was the oldest, just turned thirty, and I felt like I was going through a mid-life crisis. Both Rayana and Navi were in their late twenties, with Rayana being twenty-eight and Navi being twenty-seven.

I got out of the car, took a deep breath, then smiled. This was something I always did to mask the stress I felt like I was under. I didn't bother to knock instead; I just walked into the house. "Hey!" I said excitedly.

"Hey, Zari," Rayana said, coming from the living room.

Rayana was the one who seems to have her shit together. She found herself in nursing. She always loved helping people, finding joy in being by someone's side in a time of need. Navi found joy in snooping around and being in people's business. Her career path scared my mother but put happiness in my father's heart. He was a retired detective.

I made my way into the living room, where my father sat in his favorite chair watching the game, and Navi was sitting on the couch, going through her phone.

"Hi, Daddy, Navi," I spoke.

My father didn't even bother looking at me. "Hey baby," he mumbled.

I rolled my eyes as I made my way to where my mother was. She moved around the kitchen, cooking with love. I could hear her talking as I approached her, kissing her on the cheek. "Finally, you showed up."

I rolled my eyes as I sat at the table. "Girl, get yo butt up and set the table dinner is almost done," my mother spat.

I began doing what she asked. Rayana came in to help me. Once we were done, we'd all gathered around the table. My mother prayed over the meal, and we began eating. The sounds of the forks clinking against the plates agitated me.

"Zari, when are you coming out of this phase you're in?" she asked, waving her fork at me.

She hated that I was what people would call an earth girl. I enjoyed my so-called *phase*. I was authentically myself.

Navi turned to my mother. "I don't think it's a phase. I like it. She's free-spirited." She smiled at me.

I was happy my sister had my back. "Yeah, a free-spirited therapist who comes to her clients relaxed, allowing them to relax and open up more," Rayana chimed in.

I had a degree for it, but little did they know I wasn't using it. To their knowledge, I was doing therapy sessions and running a business. When, in fact, all I was doing was running a business. I owned a small juice book bar. Where I sold healthy drinks that included a space for reading and relaxing. My business was doing okay, but considering there was a better juice bar similar to mine, which was only a couple of blocks over, I wasn't getting the business I should have.

My phone chimed, alerting me I had a message. When I glanced down at my phone, I almost choked on my food. "What the hell!" I mumbled.

"Is everything okay, baby girl?" my father asked.

I glanced up with all of them watching me. I didn't know whether to break down and cry or rush out of the house. "I-I got to go," I told them.

"Wait! We just started dinner," my mother said, placing her hand on mine.

I took a deep breath. "I'll stay," I told her.

She smiled. I didn't want to disappoint her, but I was ready to get the fuck out of here. "You know if there is anything I can do—"

"No, I got it!" I spat at Navi.

All she wanted to do was be nosy. She did enough of that with her job. I didn't need her in my business.

"I want you all to come to church with me. I heard Dr. Kingston is giving a sermon, and I want to go."

Rayana started laughing, but my mother cut her eyes at her. "You think it's funny, but I think all three of you can use a little Jesus."

I was going to need Jesus, his bible, and his soldiers when I left here because I was on the verge of killing somebody.

CHAPTER TWO

PREACH

Pretty & The Beast

We met up at the Zoo today because we had a big shipment coming up and needed to make sure everything was in order. Everyone was here, but Chevy, shit was quiet, and it was becoming awkward because what we needed to talk about, we weren't, and it was bothering me.

"Y'all niggas going to sit around here acting mute, or are we going to address the elephant in the room?" I asked.

Zu stopped what he was doing, looking at me. I raised my brow to him. "What!" he shouted.

"Nigga how are we going to fix this. Chevy is leaving, and he's not fucking with none of us," I said.

Diamond stood walking a gun over to Foe, who was disassembling them and putting them back together. "Shit, what can we do? Y'all know Chevy's head is harder than a brick. The nigga not changing his mind about leaving."

"I know. So, are we riding with him or not?"

Foe's head shot up. "I'm down, but he's not fucking with us like that."

We all looked at Zu. He ran his hand through his dreads. The nigga was letting his pride get in the way. It was part of the reason he was in the situation now.

"I'll try to talk to him, but he not going to listen to me."

"Call Harvey," Foe jumped in.

Diamond chuckled. "She isn't talking to that nigga Zu either."

Zu shot him a look. Diamond shrugged. "What nigga, it's true. You fucked that up too."

Zu slammed his hand on the table. "Diamond, you got one more joke before I jump on yo ass. Let's not forget all three of you nigga's chose pussy over the Zoo, and one of your bitches snitched."

Zu had a point. This wasn't all on him. I pushed my glasses up on my nose, pointing to Zu, "You got a point. Harvey, though, she is closer to Chevy."

Foe stood up, "I'll call her. Tell her to come down here. The only way we are getting through to Chevy is her. Whether we like it or not, she's going to be the piece we need."

Zu stared at Foe, and he stared at Zu. "Hold the fuck on! What you mean you calling her like you got her shit stored in your phone."

This shit with Harvey was going to get ugly and fast. Zu had finally fallen for someone, a person that didn't fall for his bullshit and Foe, the shit just fell in his lap. "Man, Zu, chill out. Let's not forget she called the nigga to help her out; that's how he got the number," I jumped in looking at Foe.

I saw that shit in his eyes. He liked Harvey. When he called her number, she answered that muhfucka on the first ring. He told her to come down to the Zoo. I could see Zu side-eyeing Foe. I shook my head. I wanted to see where Foe's head was at with this Harvey situation.

"Aye, Foe, let's roll to the store real fast before she gets here."

He nodded. We jumped on our bikes and rolled out. I didn't waste a second getting to the point. "You like her, don't you?"

I said as I zoomed between cars. He didn't say nothing. When we got to the red light, he looked at me. "Like who?"

"Nigga I'm not dumb, Harvey."

Green light. He took off.

"Nah, she just cool people."

"God knows you're lying. You prayed about it?"

"Aye, Preach, leave it alone."

I laughed. *Red light.* While we waited for the light to turn green, I glanced at the car beside me, and it was the girl who was looking for me at the party.

Green light, go.

"Aye, I'm about to follow this car. I'll meet up with you back at the Zoo. God said you lying, though. You like Harvey," I said as I made a right along with the car.

"Fuck you!" I heard him as he continued straight.

I followed her as she rode through the streets. The further she went; I began to get a sense of where she was headed. When she'd finally stopped. So did I. She got out of the car walking up to the building's door. I took my helmet off and began approaching her. "The son of a preacher but a man of the streets," she said as she turned to face me.

She was beautiful. Her dark cocoa skin against the setting of the sun was one of the purest things I've seen. Her soul-searching eyes were deep brown, cheeks chubby but fitting, and her shape to me was perfection. Wide hips, thick thighs, and a fupa that was more than enough to grab onto. She extended her hand, "Navi," she smiled.

When she did that, a dimple in one of her cheeks exposed itself.

"Preach," I replied, accepting her handshake.

"You mean Prentice?"

My brow raised. "How do you know my name?"

She glanced down at her feet. "Hey, eyes on me," I told her.

"Everyone knows who you are. Your father is a known preacher in the neighborhood," she said as she looked up at me. "How do you juggle this," she paused, pointing to my father's church behind her. "And being a part of the Zoo Boyz?"

"Ask God, baby, not me," I shot back.

She nodded. This was the second time she just randomly popped up. She was now on my radar, but something was telling me this situation wasn't a Simone one. "You believe in God?" I asked.

She shrugged. "Does God exist?"

I stepped closer to her. "Clearly, he does; he created you."

I could see her shy away. "Don't be shy," I said, placing my finger to her chin, lifting it so she could look at me with those pretty brown eyes. "You weren't shy when you followed me. Nor were you shy popping up at my father's church. What you out here doing the Devil's work because it sure isn't the Lord's."

"I'm out here because I want to be."

I like how she could keep up. Normally, I would walk away from someone like her, but I had a feeling Navi had come around for a reason. Whether she was an angel in disguise, I was going to find out.

I place prayer hands to my lips. "Navi," I said. "May I take you out?"

She placed her hands on her wide hips. "What, are we doing bible study or something?"

I pointed at her, laughing. "You are funny. No, we aren't going to bible study. The type of studying I want to do doesn't got anything to do with God."

She pulled her phone out, and so did I. We exchanged numbers. Navi thought she had one up on me, but I was a child of God. Baby girl didn't know who she was really fucking with. I jogged back over to my bike when I got a text from Diamond telling me that Harvey had arrived. I knew I needed to get back before shit popped off.

Whatever storm God was brewing up, I needed to be ready.

I drove off, heading back to the precinct. I was two years in after making detective. For my father, it was excitement. For me, it was hell. Being a female detective wasn't easy, especially being black. I wanted to make my father proud, and so far, it has been working in my favor. If it were up to me, I would have chosen a different path. Not that doing what I did was a terrible thing, I just had a different dream for myself. My sisters have great careers and seem to be so happy, me I had to put on a façade.

When I received this case, I knew I had to dive in headfirst. If I could close the loop on this, then it would place me at a higher ranking, really setting the bar high for future Black female detectives. To have Prentice falling into my trap made me one step closer. I had him right where I wanted him. The gang and guns unit had been keeping their eyes on the Zoo Boyz. We had an informant, but somehow, he ended up dead. I knew the only way we were going to get more information on June Calloway was through his crew. So, my lieutenant put me undercover.

June, also known as Chevy, had already caught the team's attention before they assigned the case to me. It was documented that he had not only constructed a gun empire worth millions of dollars, but he was also responsible for a murder, specifically the killing of his adopted father. It was clear they needed more evidence to make it stick. It was the reason for Clarence going in as an informant. Now that he was dead and gone, it was up to me to solve the puzzle.

The deal was for him to say he was working with a much bigger dealer who needed the guns. Of course, we wanted to make sure he could seal the deal before giving him the government's money. However, what we got from the family was he was killed in a robbery gone wrong. It didn't help that he was a small-time hustler.

As I drove back, I spotted the woman who came into our precinct screaming and crying about witnessing a murder. I pulled over as she power-walked down the street. I quickly parked, getting out of my car to catch up with her. "Ms. Givens!" I called out.

She halted, swinging her head my way. "Who are you, and what the fuck do you want?"

She had a little attitude on her, but nothing I couldn't manage. "I wanted to talk to you about the Zoo Boyz."

Her eyes grew as she rushed over to me. "Don't get your shit split out here. I don't know anything!" she snapped.

"Well, that's not what you were saying the other night. Matter of fact, your exact words were Chevy murdered Nathaniel Jones," I told her.

Her eyes widened. "I-I lied. I told them I was shaken up and I couldn't remember. Listen, lady, stay the fuck away from me. I don't want any parts."

She began walking off. "Too late for that now!" I yelled.

Something or someone had her scared, and I was going to find out. This was my job, and those Zoo Boyz wouldn't stand a fucking chance.

By the time I got back to the office, I was ready to go as soon as I spotted Jackson sitting on my desk talking to everyone, telling one of his corny ass jokes. I rolled my eyes and stepped inside. He stopped talking abruptly to look at me.

"There she is. The woman whose dick is bigger than a lot of you walking around here."

"That includes you, right?" I snapped back.

Jackson stood from the desk as I sat down. He leaned over, placing his lips close to my ear. "No, the dick I have you couldn't handle, remember?"

The thought of him and me even being intimate on a drunk night made me cringe. I regretted it, and he never let me forget. As soon as he stepped away, I opened my file to see Preach's photo. A smile eased on my face. I knew it was strictly business, but it was nice meeting him. I pulled out my phone to text him.

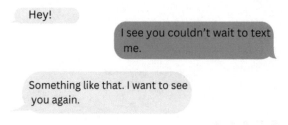

When I saw the dots appear and then go away, a feeling of him ghosting me settled in my stomach. Why did I even care if he ghosted me? This was a job. I sat my phone down, focusing back on what was important until my phone chimed again. He dropped a location, asking me to meet him at eight. A smile eased on my face. Preach had a commanding presence, and I wanted to experience it. They always say the preacher kids are the wildest ones.

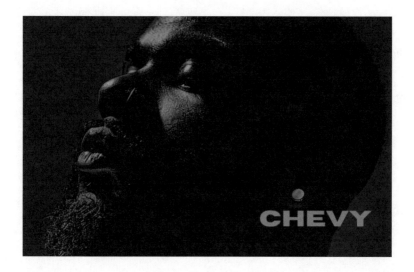

I was on my way headed to the Zoo. Today, I drove the Chevy. I needed time to think not just about my trip and relationship with my crew but also about how my demons clung on to my neck, suffocating me. My past had caught up to me, and God found a way of punishing me. I no longer had anything to live for. It seems like my bad outweighed the good I was putting into this world, and I no longer had any fucks to give. My life was headed down a road that had one ending; death. From being dealt a shitty hand since birth, starting with parents who didn't want me, to being mistreated in every single fucking home I went to. I just didn't care anymore. I was accepting my fate.

I noticed the light turning red, so I sped up, only for a woman to come running across the street, almost causing me to hit her. I slammed on the brakes, honking the horn. "Get yo ass out of the street!" I yelled out of the window.

She held up her middle finger. "Fuck you!"

I don't know why, but it triggered me. I didn't even wait for the light to change to green before I swerved right, parking in the middle of the street and hopping out. "Fuck you, you almost got your knees knocked back being fucking reckless!"

She halted, turning my way. "Who are you talking to?"

"Yo ass!"

"And it's *your* ass. Like I said before, Fuck. You. You shouldn't have been speeding anyway, fucking dick!"

"You probably need some!"

She threw her hands on her hips. "Trust me, you don't have the type of dick I'm looking for."

She turned away from me, going inside a little pissy-ass store. The fact she even challenged me made me want to run inside just to talk more shit. I got ready to hop in the car, and someone who was trying to turn honked at me. I moved quick, grabbing my gun.

Bloaw! Bloaw!

Shot each one of his tires out and drove off. I wasn't in the mood for the bullshit today. I continued until I reached the Zoo. I noticed Harvey's car parked out front, and it really sent fire through me. I did not need her being here around this shit. Every day was a battle with these niggas. A piece of new pussy comes around, and their noses are wide open. I hopped out of the car, and strolled inside. As soon as each one of them saw me, they stopped talking.

"Nah, keep talking. It's clear you niggas like celebrating without me."

Harvey smiled, "Ah, Chev, it's not like that."

"Then what is it like?"

Diamond stepped forward, crossing his arms over his chest. "I think it's funny you're mad about us talking without you present, but your ass been hiding shit from us. Now usually I'm chill, and I let things slide, but nigga what the fuck is going on with you?"

I knew they had been trying to pry for months. I wasn't ready to share that part of me yet. I had always been the one who was standing strong. I couldn't let them see me weak, not even for a mere fucking second. "I'm good. I told y'all niggas what was up. I'm leaving."

Foe chimed in. "About that. We're going with you. You told Harvey two months, and that's enough time for all of us to get our affairs in order before we leave. We're brothers. It's Zoo over everything."

"Nah."

"But Harvey can go?" Zu jumped in.

I cut my eyes at him. "Nigga not another fuckin' word."

Harvey stepped up to me. "We love you, Chevy. We just want to support you is all."

"Support me by getting this shit together. We got a fucking business to run!"

They said nothing as they finished packing up the guns. Harvey sat in the chair, just watching. Preach came close to me. "You coming to church tomorrow?"

I gritted my teeth. "God can't save a hood nigga like me."

"He saved me," he said.

"How much did he save when you're in the streets and the pulpit?" I retorted.

He looked at me and nodded. "He's a forgiving God. I promise if I wasn't saved, I would hurt you off that comment alone. You need to find Jesus!"

"You need to get back to work."

Preach glanced at me, snatching his jacket up. "Nigga I'm gone!"

Preach was my nigga, a very solid one at that. Me being honest about his straddling the fence was true. However, I knew he meant well. Shit wasn't supposed to be happening like this. My crew was supposed to be solid and unbreakable. I felt like every time we were in one room, the shit was falling apart by the second.

I walked over to Foe because I needed to get out of here. I felt like I was suffocating. "Yo, handle this for me. I'm going to step out for a second," I told him.

I could see Zu watching me and Harvey watching him. "Keep your eyes on her. If that nigga starts with the shits, get her out of here."

Foe nodded, and I headed out. A nigga just needed to breathe for a minute.

After leaving my parent's house, I went straight to the juice bar. From Cortez taking all my savings out of my bank account, to damn near being hit by a crazy ass driver, who had the audacity to talk shit afterward, I needed a break. I felt like my walls were closing in, and I wanted to be free. If the word façade was a person, I would be the poster child. My business was barely holding on. I hesitated to use my degree because I doubted my suitability to be someone's therapist when my life wasn't in order. My parents wanted perfection, and both my sisters were displaying it.

I glanced around, realizing nobody was even in the damn store. I sent my worker Mia home for the day. There was no need for her being here because who was she serving? When she left, I texted Cortez and told him to meet me here. He and I needed to talk. Cortez was a man I thought I needed in my life. He was the bad boy every girl wanted. Fine, dressed well, and hood. I'd met him at a *Love and Light festival*. It was one place I enjoyed going to every year. The sun would shine so perfectly amongst my cocoa skin. The music was a mix of Afro-punk and soul. It was such a vibe.

I was in the middle of going on a trip when Cortez approached me. His almond skin against the sun made him radiate something special. Or maybe I was just high off shrooms. He said all the right words in that moment, and I fell for it. He had stomach-length dreads, a body I thought was pure, and a mind I felt was as free-spirited as mine. His deep brown eyes screamed he was the man of my dreams, and he held a smile that went well against the sunlight. Well, all of it was bullshit. Cortez was a broken man who preyed on women he could use. He did not have money; he was fucked up and clearly a fucking thief. *No more hood niggas for me.* A hood nigga and an earth girl were two different worlds. I don't know what I was thinking. I wanted a connection. Our souls needed to match, taking up each other's energy. Cortez and I didn't have any of that.

I'd just come from the back because I had forgotten to turn the open sign off. As I made my way to the door, someone was coming in. "Sorry, I'm closed."

He stepped further inside, glancing around. "Something told me to come in here. Did I know you were going to be in here? No," He paused as his eyes landed on mine. "You ran in front of my car and had the nerve to talk shit. So yes, I came back."

The seriousness he held on his face scared me. However, he was one of the finest men I've seen in a long time. Cortez was handsome, but this was a different type of fine. Nineteen ninety fine. Dark as midnight, skin of a king, eyes of pain, and the stature of a God. The nose ring and neck tattoos added a hint of fly to him. My eyes rested on his until he pulled them away. Although he was handsome, he was still carrying the audacity he seemed to have earlier. I bet the piece he carried between his legs was of gold. He looked like if he fucked you, he would leave you soulless, stuck, and deprived.

I glanced over his shoulder, pointing to the door he had been so eager to walk through. "The door!"

He ignored what I said and began walking around, "Juice bookstore, cute."

"Excuse me?"

Eyes on me. He slowly licked his lips as his eyes traveled from my feet back to my eyes. "You need to spice shit up in here. Add plants, a little orange color to make it pop. Did you know orange represents transformation?"

THE STREETS & THE PULPIT

I crossed my arms over my chest. Who was he to come in here trying to tell me how to run my goddamn business? "For a man with a mouth like yours, I'm surprised you know something, but my—"

"Sweetheart," he held his hand up, cutting me off. "I know more than you can imagine. That's the problem; you see someone you probably think is what you women call, a *hood nigga?* And think we know nothing, or we have nothing," he said as his feet continued to pace around until he reached my bookshelf. He touched a book, pulling it out. "*Sula?* How a dark secret, no matter the bond, can come back to haunt you." He placed the book back.

He picked up another one. "*Chakara Healing.* What do you know about that?" He put it back, running his finger along the line of books, "but let me guess, you like books like this; he stopped pulling out another book, one of my favorites, Thong *On Fire.* "Hood shit? A broken woman who cannot love anybody, even her own child. Runs the streets recklessly, giving her body to any nigga just to be on top. What was her ultimate demise, huh? Death." He placed the book back.

Oh, he was an ass for real. "You read, good, now go!"

He sat on the little sofa I had, pulling something out of his pocket. *Is that a blunt?* "You can't light that in here."

He stopped and looked at me. "I can do what I want."

"Nigga if you don't get out!"

"Remember you said I was being a dick. I'm just showing you what being a dick looks like. Now come sit and smoke with me. I can use the company."

I could not believe this. Who did he think he was? I stepped right in front of him. "If you wanted my attention, that's all you had to say. You don't run me. So, I'm going to say it again," I said as I took the blunt from his hand, taking a pull. I leaned forward, nose to nose, and blew the shit right in his face. "Get out!"

He sucked up the smoke so smooth I got instant flutters in my stomach. I moved away from him as he stood up. He said nothing more. He calmly headed out the door. I don't know who this man was or thought he was, but I didn't like him. My phone vibrated in my hand, with Cortez declining my meet-up.

What the fuck!

I waited outside for Navi to show up. I wasn't surprised that she texted me. However, it surprised me how fast she did. I was going to hold off on taking her out, but after the day I had, I could use the company. Chevy had me tight, throwing my religion in my face. I didn't need anybody talking to me about the decisions I made because it was something I battled all the time. The Godly thing to do would be to walk away from Zoo, but Zoo was home for me. I could never see myself turning my back on my brothers. We killed for each other, rode together, and struggled together. I would die for Zoo. That's how devoted I was to the crew.

I spotted Navi strolling up. She seemed a little nervous, but that was okay because I was about to change that. The way she was looking, I knew I would need more than a prayer to keep my hands off her. She was the one. I could feel it in my spirit. The only thing with Navi was that she was hiding something, and this was the part I didn't like. I really wasn't here for another Simone situation because I couldn't promise if she played in my face if she would see the next day, and I hated that for her.

Navi wore an all-black two-piece set that really showed off her curves. She smiled as she approached me. "Hey," she mumbled.

I glanced down at her. "You ready?"

"I think so."

I smiled. "You don't have a choice, to be honest. Come on," I said to her as I placed my hand to the small of her back.

When she moved in front of me, her perfume clung to my nose. I closed my eyes, inhaling deeply. "God give me strength," I muttered.

I had something nice planned for her. I'd always been a man of romance. I liked the finer things, especially when I was courting. In my eyes, every woman wanted a man that would show out for them, and that's exactly what I was about to do. Once inside the restaurant, I took her by the hand, leading her toward the stairs. Navi pulled back, "Wait? We're not going to sit down here?"

"You got to trust me. Let me lead, Pretty," I said to her.

She gave a tight lip smile. I gently took her hand as we went up the steps. As we reached the top, I could see her eyes widen. "Preach!" she squealed. "You did all this for me?"

She placed her hand to her chest as she turned toward me. "Yes, yes, Pretty, I did."

We were on the rooftop that overlooked the city, capturing the beautiful parts of LA. One table, one candle, and a bouquet that held seven dozen lilies. Seven has always been a special number for me. She slowly eased toward the table. She stopped, then spun toward me.

"I've never had anyone go all out like this for me before."

"It's a first time for everything."

I walked over, pulling the chair out for her. She sat down, smiling from ear to ear. I walked over and sat across from her. I reached out for her hand, "Thank you for accepting this date, Pretty; I'm honored."

I tilted my head to the side because something in her face told me she wanted to say something.

"What is it?" I asked.

She pulled her hand away. "I-I don't know what to say."

I leaned back, crossing my arms over my chest. "Say what you're feeling. I like honesty."

"How are you friends with the Zoo Boyz? You seem so different. I heard crazy things about your crew."

I squinted now, leaning forward. "Just because you think my crew is bad doesn't mean we're bad guys. Now you're passing judgment. We all have unique personalities. Me, I'm just a man who loves God and tries his best to do what's right. Women, I cherish them. I'm a protector," I told her.

She nodded. Moments later, a server came upstairs. When I saw who it was, my initial reaction was to flip the table and snap. Instead, I played it cool. Simone approached us, looking just as shocked to see me as I was to see her.

Her eyes landed on me, then Navi. She cleared her throat, and my eyes never wavered. "I'm Simone, your server this evening, can I—"

"Two bottles of your most expensive champagne," I jumped in.

Her head flew back. "Also, once they bring the bottles up. We won't need service for a while."

I could see she was trying to talk through her eyes, but I didn't give a damn. Her best option would be to hop along and say a prayer thanking God that I didn't nut the fuck up.

"But don't you want to—"

"God bless you, Simone, is it?"

She nodded, turning around to go back to where she came from. Navi looked at me curiously but said nothing. She sat her purse down and stood. "I'm going to find the ladies' room."

I nodded. She swayed her way back down the steps. Once she was out of sight, I picked up her purse to move it away from the candle, but it slipped from my hands, and when I saw what slipped out. I shook my head.

"Lord, I ask for strength. Amen"

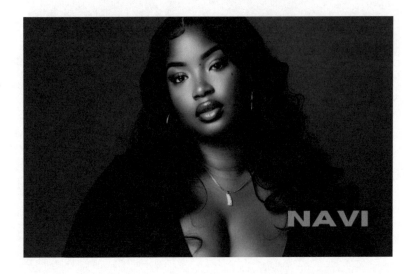

I needed to step away from the table for a second because I wasn't ready for the pressure Preach was applying. I needed to get my emotions in check because, in the end, this was a job. As I entered the bathroom, Simone entered behind me.

"He's not who you think he is," she blurted out.

I turned my head to give her my attention. "Excuse me?"

"Preach!" she yelled. "He's not who you think he is. He's confused, and with the type of things he does, he will add a little God in it to throw you off."

I really wanted her to elaborate, but I didn't want to blow my cover. However, on the flip side, she seemed bitter that he was on a date with me.

"How do you know?" I asked.

She began pacing the floor, "Because I was in your shoes. Then he fucked me and left me alone, and I-I—"

I held my hand up. "Wait, you two were together?"

She blew out a heavy breath, then rolled her eyes. "Bitch, are you listening to me? I said—"

"Simone, get back to work!" A lady popped her head into the bathroom.

I know she wanted to say more, and I wanted her to, but she just left the bathroom. I needed to get her information. That's when I realized I'd left my purse. *Shit!* I rushed out of the bathroom. When I got back to the rooftop, Preach was standing against the transparent glass that overlooked the city. My eyes landed on my purse, which was untouched exactly where I had left it.

He didn't bother to turn to me. "Come here," he said.

I eased my way up to him, placing my hand to his back, leaning my back against the glass. "You, OK?" I asked.

"I'm fine, Pretty, you good?"

"Yes."

Preach's head swiveled my way. He leaned in, kissing my forehead, then my nose. "Pretty," he called out as his hand ran up my thigh and around my stomach, pulling me closer.

"Yes?"

Preach had gone from being Mr. Soft Guy to Mr. Aggressive. His eyes bore into mine as lust filled them. The more he stared, the more I was turning into putty. I had always been in control in situations like this, but the way this man's demeanor was, I was folding and folding fast.

"God told me you were coming, and because I trust him, I'm trusting you. So, if you have anything you need to tell me, please tell me now," he practically growled.

Was Simone right? My mouth opened slightly, but nothing came out. His hand clung to my skirt, easing it up slowly. His hand caressed my leg, but his eyes stayed fixated on me. "Wha-what you want to fuck me or something?" I uttered.

He smiled. His smile was making my pussy wet. I wanted him to stop fucking smiling.

"Pretty, I'm going to fuck you, just not tonight, but these fingers will," he said as two of his fingers invaded my thong, entering me.

I gasped loudly as my head fell back, sucking in the night's air. "Ah," I moaned. "Oo, I- we shouldn't be doing this here," I mumbled.

"We do it where I say we do it. Look at me," he called out.

I wanted to, but I couldn't. I didn't know if I felt embarrassed that I was letting this man finger fuck me on the rooftop or in a bliss I couldn't get out of. My body shuddered as he slowed it down. Preach made sure he stroked every inch of my walls. He leaned forward, placing his mouth on mine, and the way he kissed me immediately told me this man was nasty. His two fingers portrayed a *come here* motion, sending me into a trance.

"Pretty, I want you to cum and cum good. You hear me?"

My mouth had been open so long that it had become dry. I licked my lips, trying to get my bearings together. "Look at me!" he barked.

My head shot up. "Cum for me," he whispered.

Now, I didn't care. I rocked my hips to keep up with him. *Eyes on him.* His pace went slower, and I lost my mind. My eyes fluttered, my body tingled, I was cummin. I grabbed his wrist, and he moved slower. My hips moved, riding his two fingers like I was riding dick. It felt so good.

"I'm cummin," I cried.

"That's right, Pretty all over my hand."

"Ah, my Go—"

He removed his hand, taking those two fingers, licking them, then sticking them in my mouth, and kissing me at the same time. This man was something serious. He was nothing like I thought. Even though it was business, I was enjoying it.

He pecked my lips a few times. When he pulled away, he fixed my skirt. Preach kissed my nose, then winked. "Next time, don't use God. He has nothing to do with this, you hear me?"

All I could do was nod. Preach was into God. This was a fact, but the man was off the chain, and I was hooked instantly.

How was I going to separate my job from this? I didn't know what I was going to do, but I wasn't giving him up. Not yet, at least.

CHAPTER
THREE

CHEVY

Loo Boyz vs Bitches

My head leaned back on the couch as I tried to get my mind in a place it needed to be. I could feel Lola gripping my dick in her hand. I placed the blunt to my lips as I stared up at the ceiling, trying to get lost in it. *How did my life end up like this?* I thought to myself. Before my mind trapped me, my head shot up. Right as Lola was about to place her lips on me, I stopped her.

She looked at me in confusion. "Did I do something wrong?"

"Lola, I need you to leave, sweetheart. This," I said, pointing between the two of us. "It isn't it. Why are you trying so hard?"

I could see her getting angry, but I didn't care. I was not about to force myself to be with someone to make them happy. Lola simply wasn't my type. She was a bird brain who couldn't see the signs if they smacked her in the face. She leaned forward, placing her elbows to my knees. "June I—"

My face balled up. "Fuck you just say?"

She jumped back. I'd never told her my real name, so her saying it told me someone either told her, or she'd been snooping through my shit.

"I-I said June, that's your name, right?"

"How the fuck do you know that?"

"I saw your mail, and I—"

I dropped my head. "You got to go. Get yo ass up, grab your Shaq heels, and leave!" I roared.

She hurried. "You are a fucking grouch. I see why you don't have anybody. Fuck you!" she shouted back.

"That's what you wanted but didn't get, big feet. Get the fuck out my shit," I stood now, towering over her.

She rushed out of the door. I knew by tomorrow she would be on the next nigga. Her calling me a grouch bothered me. I wasn't a grouch. I was just over the bullshit. I didn't have time to waste, and she was a waste of my time. I walked over to where I usually set the mail because I thought I had removed it all from that area. When I saw the piece of mail that was there, it really made me mad. Lola had opened my shit and the one thing I'd been able to keep from people she now knew. "*Fuck!*"

When I swung the door open to catch her ass, Preach was standing there. I quickly grabbed the mail, balling it up in my hand. "Sup?"

"Want to pray about it?"

"Preach, don't come here with that shit."

"What? I'm telling you, prayer works wonders. Nigga, I can assure you God is just waiting on you to talk to him so he can help you."

I was two seconds from kicking this nigga out. "You came to give me a sermon; if so, I don't need it."

He walked around me, sitting on the couch. "Nah, I came to talk to you about some shit."

"Aight, then talk."

Preach placed his elbows to his knees. "Man, maybe you do need some pussy cause you uptight as hell."

To hear him say some shit like that was a shocker to me. I sat in the chair across from him. "Talk to me."

"First, we got to figure out who snitched. Second, the laws are on to us, and I—"

"What you mean?"

"It means a woman came searching for me. I took her out only to find out she a fucking cop."

When he said that, I knew what it was about; it had nothing to do with Zoo but everything to do with me. I didn't care how upset I was at them. I couldn't let them be a part of this. "What's her name?"

Preach looked at me with a blank stare. I held my hand up. "Wait, did you fuck her?"

"I don't kiss and tell."

These niggas and their choice of women were killing me. "Tell me what the fuck is up so I can help you? Look, Chev, you've been a big brother to all of us. We're trying to be there for you the same way you were for each of us. Let us. Zoo over everything," he said.

I knew it was time to tell them what was up. I didn't want to, but I needed to. I stood up, walking over to him. "Have them niggas meet me at the Zoo tomorrow night. I want every single one of those bitches there. Including Triece's bald-headed ass."

Preach stood as well. We did our shake, and he headed out. If the laws were looking for me, I wasn't going down without guns blazing. I had two months before I left. Time was ticking. I had no time to waste. It was really time to shake shit up.

Cortez not showing up when I asked him, only showed me how guilty he was. By the time I got home, I thought he would be there, but his ass never came home. I waited up all night in the living room for him to walk through the door. I rehearsed all night what I was going to say. I glanced at the clock to see I only had about thirty minutes to get ready to meet my family at church. As bad as I wanted to call my mother and tell her I wasn't coming, I knew it would only disappoint her.

I dragged my feet so that I could get ready. I hopped in the shower to clear my head. The sound of the front door closing let me know Cortez had finally come home. I damn near broke my neck to hop out of the shower. I quickly snatched up the towel, wrapping it around myself. When I opened the door, he walked past me like I wasn't even standing there. I had a feeling he had been out with another female. She could have his ass. First, I wanted my fucking money back.

I poked my head out of the bathroom. "Hello!" I shouted.

He stopped, turning to me, smiling. "What's up, babe?"

What's up, babe? "Where were you?"

He ran his hand over his face. "I was out with the guys got tied up with some shit."

I knew he was lying. "Cortez cut the shit. Where the fuck is my money?"

He went from calm to defensive. "I don't know what you're talking about."

I rushed out of the bathroom, getting in his face. "Nigga you're the only one who has access to my account. Now, where the. Fuck. is. My. Money!" I belted.

He brought his face closer to mine. Before he even said a word. I sniffed and sniffed hard. "I know damn well you didn't come into my fucking house after eating pussy."

He turned to walk away.

"Get out. Get all your shit and get the fuck out my house now!"

"I'm not going anywhere."

"You're getting the fuck out of here!"

Cortez spun so quickly that I jumped back into the wall. "What you gone do? Huh? Go in there, grab your fucking rocks and sage to cast a spell on me or some shit. Zaria, we're locked in, and I'm not going anywhere. Oh, and that money. It's fucking mine. I need it more than you!"

Who did he think he was playing with? I clenched onto my towel, drew my hand back, and slapped his ass. His head swung and slowly came up. "First pass next time, I'm going to knock you on your ass," he gritted.

"I hate you. You took everything I had, and you're standing here in my face after one, fucking some bitch, and two stealing my money, ha," I said, now heading toward the room. "I got something for your ass. Hold that thought."

I hurried and tossed my dress on. I rushed to my drawer, grabbing my gun. I ran out of the room, swinging my gun down the hall. Cortez was gone. *Fuck!*

I didn't know what I was going to do. With the money he had taken, it was all I had to keep my business afloat until the business pulled in the money it needed. Tears instantly welled in my eyes because it was only a matter of time before I lost my business. I sat on the floor, crying my eyes out. I can't believe I allowed this man to use me like this. I could have told my parents, but I was too ashamed to even let them know what was going on. I needed a fucking break. I was going to get my money back, and when I did. I was out of here.

I needed a fresh fucking start, but first, I needed some information. I hated to do it, but I needed Navi's help.

"Amen," my father said as he had just finished prayer before ending the service.

Everyone said their farewells as they exited the church. I stood around as I usually did, speaking to the youth and deacons. I could see my father eyeing me from where he stood. I knew he wanted to ask when I would step up, but I just wasn't ready. Diamond came up to me. "I'm going to take my granny home, and I'll meet y'all at the Zoo. They found the girls," he whispered.

I nodded. I could see my father approaching over Diamond's shoulders. Before he could get away, my father placed his hand on Diamond's shoulder. Diamond's eyes widen. *Get yo daddy, nigga.* He mouthed.

I dropped my head, pinching the bridge of my nose, trying to hold in my laugh.

"Brother Diamond. You know we could use you in the choir. With that voice you have, you should be singing for the lord."

"I should be getting out of here."

My father chuckled. "Don't run from your calling," he said, looking at me.

Diamond walked off, leaving me standing there. He turned to look at me. *That nigga's crazy.* He mouthed.

"Prentice, have you thought about what I said?"

I shook my head. "I really don't think I can do it. I'm still kind of—"

"Proverbs chapter three verse five and six."

"Trust the Lord with all your heart and not lean on your own understanding," I recited.

"Then you know what to do," he finished, backing away.

I was really struggling. This may have been one of the hardest decisions I'd ever have to make. I headed out of the church to see Navi standing there. I spotted her in church today with what I assume was her family.

"So, you really are a church boy," she smiled.

I reached out for her hands. "Pretty, it was good to see you in service today."

"Yeah, something my mom asked us to do. I honestly don't believe in God."

"Better start believing Pretty if you want to be with me. Don't wait until a moment in need to believe in him do it now. I promise, baby, he's the only one who's going to save you," I said as I kissed her forehead and began walking away.

"Where are you going?" she yelled out.

"To handle business, Pretty, we'll get up later. Have a blessed day," I told her.

Navi was cool. Although she was a cop, I didn't have solid facts that she was around to cause havoc in my life. God said there will be a storm, and she had to be it. Now, I had to let things play out because as bad as I hated to do it, if I needed to, Navi would end up meeting her God, which was the Devil himself.

***

The sounds of sobs filled the Zoo. "One two, the Zoo Boyz coming for you," Diamond started.

"Three, four, the hoes better lock their doors," Foe jumped.

I clapped. "Five, six, we came to shake up shit!"

Diamond walked up. "Seven, eight better come at us straight."

In unison, Foe, Diamond, and I finished. "Nine, ten, can you see us coming."

"Diamond, please, I swear I didn't say anything," Monette cried.

Diamond flicked his nose as he stood in front of her while her body swung from the ceiling. He reached out to her, caressing the side of her body, "I warned you, Mo," he told her.

Foe sat back in the chair, watching all four girls hanging from the wooden post bucking wildly.

"Foe, this some fuck shit. Nigga why would I snitch on you?" Asia gritted. "You know I'm not even like that!"

Foe shrugged, "I honestly don't give a fuck, my love. One or all of you are a snitch, and not one of you leaving this bitch until we find out."

Simone's cries became louder. I circled the girls. "I hope y'all prayed today. Another day, I got to backslide because y'all Jezebels tried the gang."

Diamond began singing, taunting the girls. *"Cry me a river, cry me, cry me."*

The only one who hadn't said a word was Triece. She hung in silence. "Aye, Triece, I didn't see you in church; what happened?"

"Fuck you, Preach. You are going straight to hell!" she screamed.

"God's, my judge, not you, but if I did go to hell, I'll be right next to yo ass."

The doors to the warehouse opened and not only did Chevy come in, but he had three of Triece's brothers. What surprised me was Harvey behind him. She looked super nervous and out of place. Chevy was unpredictable. You never knew what this nigga was conjuring up. Moments later, Zu entered.

"Baby, why are you here?" he asked Harvey.

She shrugged. "Chevy asked me to come."

Zu peered at Chevy. "What nigga? Y'all want her around so bad. Y'all know the rules: we don't touch women or kids. But Harvey can," he said as he slid his jacket off.

Chevy had lost all his mind. Foe jumped up, "Nigga what? She ain't doing this shit!"

He spun toward Foe. "Fuck you gone do about it, huh!" Chevy barked. "Harvey's a big girl. Let her decide. The way you talking like you her nigga or is that her nigga?" he pointed to Zu.

Chevy was completely losing his shit by the day. "Now, back to business." He walked toward the girls. "I got my little demon today, ladies," he calmly said. "Harvey, get the whip."

We all looked at Harvey, who stood there and didn't move. "Harvey, get the fucking whip!" Chevy barked.

Triece's laugh filled the warehouse. "Zu, and this the bitch you want. Tuh, I don't why—"

THE STREETS & THE PULPIT

Whiplash!

"*Ah!*" her body arched in the air as she screamed.

Whiplash!

Harvey swung the whip across her back again. "Say something else bitch!"

Triece's head flung back with her mouth wide. "Looks like she's begging for Jesus now," Diamond said.

I cut my eyes at him.

Whiplash!

The sound whistled through the warehouse. You could hear the whip connecting with Triece's back, splitting her flesh open. Simone was losing her shit by the second. Chevy began clapping hard and loud. "Yeah, got my little demon on go! Again Harvey!"

Whiplash!

Triece body trembled. Zu rushed over to Harvey, snatching the whip out of her hand. "Give me this shit."

"So, you taking up for her?" Harvey snapped.

Zu dropped his head. "No, I would never do that, but you shouldn't be doing our dirty work. This is not your lane."

Rat tat tat tat! Rat tat tat tat!

Triece's screams got louder. We all turned to see one of her brothers being fried by Chevy's bullets. "Now, are we going to have another episode of Love and Hip Hop or get some shit done?"

He swung the gun at Triece. "I warned your flintstone-looking ass. It was you who snitched, and because I can't do shit to you, them niggas," he used the choppa to point to her brothers. "They ass about to be lit up like hot fuckin' soup. One down, two to go." He winked.

All the girls wailed loudly. The shit was becoming annoying. I couldn't take it.

Bloaw!

I shot in the air. "Shut the fuck up! Y'all need to be speaking in tongue, asking God to save y'all. Now Triece, what the fuck did you say!" I shouted.

Diamond and Foe walked over to her brothers, aiming a gun at each one. "I've been waiting to shoot one of these niggas," Foe said.

Triece closed her eyes as the tears rolled down her face. Before she could say anything, Harvey snatched the whip from Zu.

Whiplash!

"*Ah!*"

"Speak up, hoe. You had a lot to say before!" Harvey shouted.

Zu picked Harvey up, throwing her over his shoulder. "Chill the fuck out! I don't want you a part of this, please!"

"Fuck you, Zu, you probably still fucking her."

It was clear they hadn't made up since the race. The way Zu was acting was something I'd never seen. Usually, he was with the fuckery, but this was different. He truly had fallen for Harvey. She was making the nigga soft. I glanced over at Foe, who was focused on what they were doing. One of Triece's brothers got up running. I aimed and shot.

Bloaw!

One to his back. He dropped to the ground. Chevy walked over to him as he tried to crawl away. "Night nigga!"

Rat tat tat tat!

His body bounced off the floor. I bowed my head to say a prayer for him. "Heavenly Father, I pray they found peace before they took their last breath, Amen."

"I told them Chevy killed Nash!" she screamed. "Please just stop. I promise I haven't said shit else. I told them I was tripping when the lady cop came and asked me."

A bell went off in my head. *Lady cop?* Navi had been snooping around. Chevy had nothing to do with Nash. Triece lied because of her hate for him. Foe glanced at me. Chevy's head slowly turned my way, then back at Triece.

"Name, what's her fucking name!" Chevy growled.

"I-I don't know." She cried.

Chevy nodded. "Let these bitches down!" He roared.

Zu walked away from Harvey, letting each girl down but Triece. Simone glanced at me as tears rolled down her face.

This let me know she was going to be a problem, and I knew I was going to have to handle it myself. Asia moved toward the door as she peered at Foe.

"Fuck you looking at go!" he yelled at her.

I knew she wouldn't say anything because she knew the code. Asia had enough respect for Foe not to say one word. Monette rushed over to Diamond. She was in love with my nigga. It was all over her face, but she had been the main reason for everything happening the way it did. She walked out with her head down, and Simone hauled ass out after her. We were left with Triece and one of her brothers. Zu walked over to Triece. "You know we can't let you go, right?"

Triece just closed her eyes, accepting her demise. Zu placed his hand around her neck and squeezed. Triece's eyes bulged the tighter Zu squeezed. It was the first time one of us had ever put our hands on a woman, but it needed to be done.

Her brother screamed. "Y'all got a church nigga in here and y'all killing people? Chevy, man, this ain't it nigga. Let my sister go!"

Bloaw!

Foe pulled the trigger. He didn't even let us respond. He was as bad as Chevy with the guns.

"Damn trigga happy nigga," Diamond said to him.

"Happy on the fucking trigga," Foe shot back.

The sound of Triece's last breath signaled she was dead. Zu released her.

"Heavenly Father, I pray they found peace before they took their last breath, Amen," I said.

"Get this shit cleaned up, and I want everybody at my house in two hours!" Chevy barked, snatching his jacket and leaving the building.

I knew I needed to get to Navi before Chevy did. This nigga was on one and wasn't letting up.

After leaving the Zoo. I was trying to decide if I was going to find this lady cop who had been lurking or if I was going to let Preach handle it. The walls felt like they were closing in, and I wasn't sure which direction I wanted to go to escape it all. I knew I couldn't run forever, but I needed just enough time to take my trip.

I sped through the streets to get back to my place. Every situation I came across in my life had been a trial. I'd been able to overcome most, whether it was by laying someone down or contributing to something for the good, yet the burden of the world still felt like it was on my back.

74

THE STREETS & THE PULPIT

I'd just come up to a red light when my eyes landed on the woman who ran the bookstore juice bar. She hurried inside her place. Something seemed off. I knew I should have just gone straight, but something about her demeanor this time looked different. I got over, riding onto the curb, and parked my bike right in front of her door. The last time I walked through her door, it was to be an ass because she had challenged me. This time, it was out of pure concern. I slid my helmet off before entering her establishment.

"I'm sorry I'm not—" She sighed loudly. "Why are you here? I really don't have time for your bullshit." Waving me off.

This time, I took her in. Shorty was cute. Naturally curly, coarse hair that sat shoulder length, hypnotizing tight dark eyes, and skin that kissed the sun a million times without being damaged. Her style was different than what I was used to. She wore an assortment of bracelets, necklaces, a nose ring, and she had an average body. Thick thighs, big breasts, a little ass and hips, with a little stomach on her. She wore a peanut butter brown crochet-type top and a skirt that sat at her hips. As I admired her beauty, I almost forgot why I'd come in here.

I moved closer to her as her eyes watched me curiously. She smelled like she slopped on the entire container of shea butter, but it was hypnotizing. "You've been crying?" I asked.

She wiped her eyes. "No, and if I was, why do you care? You were just in here days ago being a fucking asshole."

This was true. I was also a man who tried to help those who were in need. At this moment, she was in need. I reached out for her hand. "I apologize."

She snatched her hand away. "I don't need your apology. Thank you for stopping by," she said as she turned away.

I was open like a curious cat. I wanted to know more about her. "What's your name?" I asked.

She stopped spinning my way. Hurt swallowed her. I could see that shit all in her eyes. I knew personally what it felt like. She paused for a second, then snapped. "Look, I accepted your apology, but what I don't need is a smart-mouth-ass nigga like you here. This is my last time asking you to leave."

I'd never had a woman push me out before. It was me who constantly pushed others away. The world I lived in, they didn't need to be wrapped in it. I threw my hands up, backing away. All I was trying to do was help. Our eyes never wavered as I backed away. If I didn't believe in nothing else, I believed in connection. Something was telling me she was something special. The fact she didn't want me around made me want to come back. Once, I was outside. I slid my helmet on, hopped back on my bike, and took off.

***

Just like clockwork, the crew had arrived. The only person I was waiting to show up was Harvey. She needed to be a part of this conversation. I watched as Zu awkwardly stood against the door. Our conversation with each other had been at the bare minimum. I didn't know if I was ready to sit and have the one-on-one we needed. Zu fucked up a lot. Him putting my business on the line. I didn't know if I could forgive him for that.

I wanted to share a piece of my past with them, but I needed each of them to understand that just because I was being transparent didn't mean I would step back and ride with Zoo. My life had shifted, and there were more important things I needed to worry about, such as the laws that were clearly on my ass. I could see Diamond tapping Preach's arm, pointing at Zu, laughing.

"Zu, nigga sit down," he cackled.

"I'm straight."

I stepped over to Zu, pointing toward the living room, "Nigga sit down."

Zu moved away from the wall, coming up to me like he wanted to buck. We were eye to eye. *"Ah, shit!"* I heard Foe, who had now moved closer to Zu and me.

See, what they didn't understand was Zu and me. We were different, older, and far wiser. Zu still had some growing to do.

THE STREETS & THE PULPIT

Zu held his hand out, stopping Foe from coming closer. He directed his attention and big nigga energy toward me. I could smell it. "Nah, no need. I'm here because at the end, Chev, my nigga, you still my fucking brother," he said, pointing at my chest. "I would die for you. Hell, all you niggas. But what you not about to do is come at me like you a nigga's daddy 'cause mine is six feet in the fucking ground."

I flicked my nose, then shrugged my shoulders. "Zu, the right thing to do would be to knock yo muhfuckin top back. That's the type of time I'm on." I put my hands in my pockets because I really wanted to use them on his gorilla-looking ass. I leaned forward so he could hear me loud and clear, "I don't give a shit about nothing, and I mean that shit. You made it this way, not me. However, I'm going to have a little decorum today because what we need to talk about is bigger than your bullet head ass. So," I stepped closer. "Sit yo rabbit ass *down!*"

I turned to Foe, who stared at me like I was crazy. "Y'all need to hash this shit out. Chevy, we want you back in Zoo, bottom line."

Before I could speak, Harvey came in the house. I glanced back at Foe, then winked. They all went into the living room. I stood there watching all of them. Me doing what I was about to do was hard for me, but I knew I had to. I ran my hand over my head. "I killed my adopted father," I blurted out.

"Chev!" Harvey yelped.

I held my hand up, "Let me finish. The man was the Devil. He tortured me any way he could when I was young. Shit that will forever live in my brain. Things I could never forgive him for. He used me as a tool to win a fucking election. I was a disposable piece of trash to him. So yes, when I had the opportunity, I took it. Not only did I do that, but I also used the shit I learned from his crooked ass and started a million-dollar business that helped each of you in some way."

Diamond held a look of surprise on his face. "Is this why you're leaving? You are running from the laws?"

"I'm leaving because it's something I want to do. I need to do. Whatever my fate is, I will accept it. I just needed to tell you all so I can save you guys from the bullshit. I'm giving you an out. Right here, right now."

Preach stood. "That's not how this works. I told you God is forgiving. Your fate can change. You just don't have faith. It's Zoo over everything."

He came in, leaning close to my ear. "I like her. Let me handle it, trust me, please," he finished, pulling away from me.

"One shot," I told him.

Foe and Diamond stood. "Zoo over everything," they said in unison.

Foe pulled his gun out. "Guns fucking blazing."

Harvey stood, "I love you, Chevy. You know I got your back. I only fuck with the Zoo!" she smiled.

Zu looked at me, then at Harvey. "I got yo back, my nigga," he said, then turned to Harvey. "A nigga, sorry, I really want to be with you."

My eyes landed on Harvey, who looked at Zu, then slowly crept her eyes toward Foe. My eyes landed on Foe, whose jaws tightened as he dropped his head. That situation alone was messy, and if it didn't get resolved, Zoo would be no more. Harvey didn't reply. Instead, she just smiled at Zu.

I glanced over at everybody. Each one of them brought something to the table that I admired. They were my family, an imperfect family that had my back. It was almost bittersweet because once I went on this trip, little did they know I wasn't coming back. It was the major reason I declined my niggas offer to go.

I had just gotten home from being with my parents. I was hoping to spend a little time with Preach, but he had other arrangements. After getting comfortable, I opened the file to go over it, trying to put the pieces together since I had free time. I laid out all the pictures. I glanced at Chevy's the longest. I wanted to understand him. His picture alone spoke volumes. His eyes held pain, and I wanted his full story. The story I was hoping Preach would soon share. The Calloways adopted Chevy when he was ten years old. They weren't the type of family you would think would adopt a little, ghetto, Black boy.

They were a white, prestigious family. The father, Matthew, was a city council member trying to run for governor, but he needed the minority's vote. So why not adopt a little Black boy showing he cared about the community and our people? I shook my head at the thought. I wanted to justify what we think Chevy did because, again, we had no actual proof. It was all speculation. Did he torture Chevy? What would make him come back years later to hurt the man that took him in?

The sound of my doorbell went off, pulling me away from the case file. I pulled myself up off the floor to go to the door. When I glanced in the peephole, I saw it was Jackson. I would have loved to ignore him, but he was still my colleague. I unlocked the door, swinging it open. Jackson stood there with a smirk on his face. I could see him peeking over my shoulder.

"Working?"

I rolled my eyes. "What do you want?"

"I came to talk about the case."

He was lying, "Ok, then talk."

He pushed the door open wider, letting himself in. "Jackson, get out."

Jackson was here because he thought we were going to have another encounter like before, and that wasn't about to happen. I rushed over to my files, swooping them back into the folder and placing it on the table. Jackson's eyes traveled all over my body as he stepped toward me, making me back away.

"Jackson, go!" I yelled.

THE STREETS & THE PULPIT

"Navanna Richardson, the only female detective in the department. Black woman at that," he said, leaning forward.

My head moved back. I realized he'd trapped me against the wall. I tried shoving him off, but his body weight was too heavy.

"How did you get this job, your daddy?"

Being harassed by the men in this field was ridiculous. This is what my father didn't understand and another reason I hated my job. "If you want to keep the dick in those pants, you better get out of my fucking face," I gritted.

Jackson leaned in further now, pressing his body against mine. "You can't do shit to me. I, however, can do everything I want to—"

"Did you pray today?" Preach emerged from behind Jackson, holding a gun to his head.

I was happy he was here, but I didn't want him making the mistake of killing Jackson. It would put me in the middle and Preach behind bars.

"Preach, don't!" I yelled.

Jackson laughed. "A man of God with a gun in his hand. If you were smart, you would want to put that shit away," Jackson said as he spun around. Now, the gun was at his forehead.

Preach's eyes landed on mine. "Pretty, move out the way because when I blow this nigga's top off, I don't want the nigga's dirty thoughts on that pretty ass face."

Preach pressed the barrel of the gun further into Jackson's forehead. I began panicking. My phone began vibrating on the table. I quickly glanced down, and it was Zaria. She would have to wait. I stepped closer to Preach. Placing my hand on his, "Baby, don't do it. What would God say."

Preach glanced at me as a flicker went off in his eye. He lowered his hand, turning to me.

"Good church boy. God don't like ugly. Isn't that what you folks say?" I heard Jackson taunting him.

Preach dropped his head, bringing it up slowly, smirking. "Pretty, you better call on Jesus!" he barked. He didn't even take his eyes off me.

Bloaw!

Jackson's body flew back. I jumped, and Preach lowered the gun. I could hear Jackson groaning in the corner. Preach walked over to him, squatting down, while Jackson held his side. "I want you to repeat after me," Preach said to him.

Jackson began sweating profusely. I snatched my phone from the table. "Navanna, call fucking help!" Jackson yelled.

My hands trembled as I held the phone in my hand. Preach still hadn't looked at me. He should have run instead; he moved closer to Jackson, gripping him by his throat. "Pretty is

84

not a piece of property. She's a woman, one who deserves some respect. Now, repeat after me. Lord God," he paused.

The way he was taking up for me was making it harder to call this situation in. "Sha-she's a fucking—"

Bloaw! Bloaw!

I sent two bullets through Jackson. I wasn't going to let him ruin this case for me. Preach stood, saying a prayer for a man we'd just put bullets in. He came over to me, tapping my nose. "I guess we're both going to ask God for forgiveness, Detective Richardson." He winked.

"You let me kill him!" I screamed.

"No, you did what your heart told you to do. You would rather protect your name than be outed. It had nothing to do with me. You just committed murder, Pretty. So, before you go passing judgment, think about what the fuck you just did."

I couldn't believe this shit. He knew all along and hadn't said a fucking word. Preach walked over to the door to leave but turned to me. "Once you get this handled," he said, pointing around. "My house tonight. No panties, no bra, I'm going to fuck you tonight, Pretty," he finished, leaving my house.

I swallowed deeply. I knew I should have taken him in, but Preach talks one hell of a good game. I realized that it wasn't just Chevy who was dangerous, but all of them. They were all killers. Now it made sense why Ms. Givens was so scared. I

needed to decide if it would be me who showed up at his door
or my brothers in blue.

I'd finish settling business for my store. I chose to sell it and start traveling. It was going to be bittersweet, but I felt like it was my only option. I was already in the hole; me selling it, I would break even. I was going to tell my family, but I wanted to embrace the moment first. Knowing I no longer would have this responsibility and could live freely was a breath of fresh air. I just needed to get my money back from Cortez. Hell, I didn't know if he had spent it all, but I was going to find out.

I checked my phone to see if Navi had called me back, but she hadn't. It never took her nosy ass this long to call me back before. I picked up my purse to leave as a group of guys entered the store. "I'm closed."

One of them stood there smiling. It was about six of them. They wore biker jackets. It brought me back to the guy who came into the store earlier. "If he sent y'all, I said I was fine."

One of them laughed. "We want to be serviced."

"I said I'm fucking closed, now get out!"

Another one of them walked toward my book area, allowing me to see the back of his jacket. *Blaze N' Fire.* This wasn't the same name I saw earlier. That guy's jacket said Zoo Boyz. Panic set in. *Were they here to rob me?* "I don't have any money," I blurted out.

One of them jumped over the bar, knocking things over. "We're looking for Cortez."

"He's not here, matter of fact, I don't know where he is," I told them honestly.

I saw my bookshelf slam against the floor. My eyes then bounced back on the guy in front of me. The type of luck I had, this shit would happen to me. Cortez has been trouble in my life since meeting him. The more things came to light, the more I hated. Cheating was one thing, but this shit was completely another level of evil.

Closer.

"He owes us some money, and I came to collect."

Closer.

"I-I don't have any money," I said as I tried walking around, but he stopped me.

"Get your fucking hands off me!" I yelled.

"I said—"

"She said get your fucking paws off her!" I heard another man's voice.

When I looked, it was the guy from earlier. *Thank God!* "Nigga, who are you?"

Bloaw!

I jumped, throwing my hands over my mouth when the guy who knocked over the bookshelf body went down. He held onto his leg.

"I'm your worst nightmare, and you got one peg leg rider." He came closer. "How much she owes you?"

"Fifty bands."

I couldn't believe Cortez owed fifty thousand dollars. "Let's race for it? I would assume those are your bikes outside."

The guy had now placed all his attention on my new hero. "When?"

The guy holding his leg groaned. "Nigga I can't fucking ride like this!" he screamed.

His partner looked at him, then back to the mystery man. "When?" he asked again.

"Tonight! The downtown bridge. Group race, two miles and back double or nothing."

The guy looked at me, then back at him. "Oh, you into saving bitches."

The mystery man rushed up to him, aiming a gun at his head. "We ain't doing that. You already got one nigga down. You want another one? You can accept my offer to race, or I can give her a new painting for these shitty ass walls called a stupid nigga's dream," he gritted.

Did he insult my store again?

"Race," the guy mumbled.

He and his crew headed out. "You, ok?" the mystery man asked.

"Thank you," I said to him.

Not only was he fine, but he seemed to fear nothing. There was silence as he stared at me without uttering a word. A few seconds seemed like minutes. I had more to say, but I was unsure how to articulate my thoughts. So, I smiled, but he didn't. He gave me a quick nod before leaving the store. This was the third interaction, and we still didn't know each other's names. The universe was speaking to me, and I wasn't sure if I was ready to listen. I did want to see this race, though.

I closed the store, rushing out the door to the bridge.

I waited in my living room for Pretty to show up. I had prayed for the last hour to God, hoping he would give me a sign that Navi was worth the sacrifice. It was something about her that drew me in, and I didn't want to walk away. Maybe it was her straddling between her work and me. I could relate because it is what I've been battling for years.

Foe said he would be out for a while, so I didn't have to worry about him. I watched the clock as time ticked. I was trusting she didn't fuck me over by giving up my boys and myself. I knew Chevy was trusting me, and I didn't want to let him down yet again by making the wrong decision. The sound of light taps at my door made my stomach drop. The last time I had gotten this nervous was after being caught in the bathroom with the cheerleader waiting for my father to show up.

I got up, making my way to the door. I bowed my head, saying a silent prayer before I opened the door. She stood there in a dark-brown trench coat with orange pumps on. Her hair was in a high bun, deep red lipstick, and her face held light makeup. "I trust you," she said softly.

"You look so fucking good," growled.

She strutted through the door, one foot in front of the other. I pointed to the sky. *Thank you, God.* Pretty slowly turned, opening her coat, exposing her fully naked body. I strolled over to her, tapping her nose.

"Remember, do not say God no matter how much you want to call on him. He has nothing to do with this."

She placed her hand on her hip, "I've been bad, real bad. What are you going to do about it?" she purred.

I wrapped my arms around her, gripping her ass in my hands. "Wait. I can walk to the room; you don't have to—"

I did it. I picked her up. I didn't know if she figured because she was on the thicker side, it would stop me from doing what I wanted to and with her, but she was going to learn today that her size meant nothing at all. "Let me lead, Pretty. I like all of you, every single fucking curve," I said as I pecked her on the lips.

I carried her to the room, setting her on the edge of the bed. "Turn around and get on your knees," I instructed her.

She did as I told her. Pretty's sexy ass on all fours turned me on by the second. I wanted to explore every single part of her body, even the parts she was insecure about. I went to my drawer, taking out my Zoo paddle, gripping it in my hand. I could see her head turn curiously. She went to speak, and I placed my finger to my lips. "Shh, let me lead Pretty, you just enjoy."

I drew my hand back and swung.

Smack!

Her body bucked forward. "Ouch!"

"You said you've been bad?"

Smack!

"Ah shit!" she squealed.

I moved toward her, caressing her ass. I drew my hand back again, swinging the paddle. *Smack!*

"Welcome to the Zoo, Pretty!"

Smack!

Her yelps had now turned into moans.

"Open up," I told her.

She parted her legs only slightly.

Smack!

"I said open them fucking legs, Pretty I want to see that pussy from the back."

THE STREETS & THE PULPIT

"But, Preach I—"

"Pretty open them fucking legs. Behind these doors, I'm not a saint, baby, I'm a sinner. Now open them shits wide."

Her legs move further apart, exposing her brown pussy lips. I set the paddle down, coming out of my clothes. I dropped to my knees. "Thank you for this meal, Amen," I whispered.

"Did you just pray?" I heard her ask.

I snatched the paddle. *Smack!*

"No talking."

I leaned forward, wrapping my lips around her clit that peeked through from the back. Pretty gasped so loud, then a purr rolled off her tongue. Her body moved back, but I used my hands to push her forward. I sucked on her pretty pussy so slow. For every twist, every flicker, every lap, I wanted her to feel it.

Her body began slowly moving. "Oh my—"

Smack!

I didn't want her to cum, so I removed my lips from around her. The juice from her pussy leaked on my bed. She was ready. I ran my tongue up her ass until I reached the lower part of her back. I slid my dick up and down her wet trail. Using my hands, I spread her ass cheeks apart, watching my dick disappear inside her. "Damn, Pretty, this pussy wet as hell," I grunted.

Roll up, then roll down.

94

She tried reaching behind her, so I grabbed her hand to bring her up some. I leaned forward to place my chest to her back. I used my free hand to caress her nipple. "It fe-feels so fucking good," she whined.

Roll up, then roll down.

"Fuck me, Preach, just keep fucking me," she begged.

Roll up, then roll down.

I bit into her neck, "The way this pussy feel should be criminal," I said as I sucked on her earlobe.

"Murder it then puh-lease."

Roll up, then roll down.

I sucked on her neck while I stroked her from behind. I released her. I wanted to see her face. "Turn around."

Once she turned around, I entered her again. Pretty's eyes sat low as she licked her lips. She played with her titties while I fucked her. I gripped her waist, pulling her toward the edge of the bed. I lifted only her bottom half and began digging her the fuck out.

"My God!"

"I said don't bring his name up," I gritted.

I leaned forward, kissing her while I continued.

Roll up, then roll down.

I was about to cum. She pulled her lips away. "Preach baby, oh my goodness!" she screamed as her pussy muscles gripped my dick, sending me on edge.

Roll up, then roll down.

The nut came up so fast I didn't have time to pull out. *Fuck!* I would have to pray about it later because right now, a nigga just went to ecstasy.

She got up to use the shower. I heard the front door open, so I knew it was Foe. Something in my gut told me to go check. I slipped on my shorts, heading out of the room. I saw his shoes and a female pair of shoes by the door. Not that it mattered. I was curious if he and Asia had made up. I could see the black light coming from his cracked door. I eased my way over. I peeked through the crack to be nosy. My eyes widened when I caught a glimpse.

Damn!

Downtown bridge in thirty. Race, 100 bands on the table!

Ahh shit! omw

Race? I got company. Give me a minute damn!

Preach that pussy can wait! Money on the line.

Omw! Preach too Holy for pussy.

I'm Holy but my hands not keep playin'.

Where the fuck is Zu?

👀

With Harvey maybe? 😒 Ayo Foe, you heard from Zu?

97

I didn't know where Zu was, but I hope he checked his messages. When I arrived at the bridge. A crowd for Blaze N' Fire was already there. More cars began arriving. It was people who supported us. Them niggas were terrible because they were the only who would call people to come and see us race. They needed a crowd every time. Fifteen minutes passed and I could hear their bikes approaching. *"We don't fuck with you; we only fuck with da Zoo!"* people chanted.

First Diamond pulled up, then Preach and Foe. I glanced at them as they removed their helmets. "Where the fuck is Zu?"

Diamond hit his kickstand, coming over to me. "Shit we tried calling, but he didn't answer. You probably hurt the nigga's feelings," Diamond shrugged.

"Not tonight!"

I saw Harvey pull up, so I knew he wasn't with her. *Fuck!* This was the time I didn't need Zu to let me down. Harvey strolled over to us. "Sup," she smiled.

Why the fuck was she smiling? "Where is Zu?"

The look on her face told me she wasn't with him. I reached in my pocket, giving her the orange and brown rag. "You are calling the race tonight."

She reluctantly took it out of my hand. "But Chev I—"

"Please! Preach you riding front with me, Foe middle Diamond the tail."

Foe came up. "We got it with or without Zu," he said.

Shit, we really didn't have a choice. Foe turned to Harvey. "You straight. All you got to do is swing it in the air and swing that bitch down."

I glance between the two of them. "Y'all playing with fire," I gritted.

"Why are we racing anyway, I thought you were done?"

The more they talked, the more irritated I was becoming. "Helping someone," I grumbled.

Harvey swayed her way to the center. We lined up, revving up our bikes. We slid our helmets on.

"You good Chev?" Diamond asked.

"Always!"

We all watched Harvey waiting on her signal.

"*We don't fuck with you; we only fuck with da Zoo!*" the people chanted.

"I'm here ran into some shit with Dio," I heard Zu's voice. "Damn Preach get out my spot."

"Nah nigga you late you take the tail with Diamond's singing ass."

Harvey held the flag up.

"Damn she's pretty," Zu said.

Harvey's hand swung down. "*Go!*" she screamed.

"Nigga, let's ride!" I shouted as I took off.

We zoomed down the road. Preach and I crossed lanes. I sped up leading.

"*Woo Shit!* That nigga Chev flying like a bird!" Diamond shouted.

Swerve. Lean left, swerve.

Preach sung. "Way up I feel blessed!"

Foe jumped in, laughing. "Oh yeah, Preach got some pussy."

"I got Jesus. Yes Lord!"

Gear switch, left lane, right lane. Wheely.

"Okay we see you nigga, watch this!" Foe came in again.

Foe dipped through the lanes, zooming past us, swerving his shit in a circle, building smoke, then taking off straight again. Two of the Blaze N' fire riders swerved as they came up on the smoke, taking them off course.

The sound of Zu howling filled the helmet. "Two down three bitches to go."

I couldn't lie. I loved riding. It was an adrenaline you couldn't describe. No matter the shit we went through, when it was time to ride, Zoo stayed solid. I just wished this shit could last forever. We'd come to where we had to turn around. My head began spinning. My vision started becoming blurry. *Shit!* "Focus nigga come on," I whispered to myself.

"You good Chev?" Preach asked.

"I'm straight."

I had to end this race. I switched gears and took off. I began picking up speed. *Seventy, eighty, ninety,* the speedometer went up. I could barely see the crowd. I couldn't tell if I was getting closer or not. Until I heard Preach. "Ayo Chevy slow the fuck down!"

I screeched my tires; my blinking became rapid. That's when I noticed how close I was to hitting Harvey. I swerved hard, leaning on my bike only inches from the ground. The sound of my tires pierced my ears. I swerved enough to miss her by a hair. I came up halting my bike, sending my back tire in the air, then slamming down.

"We don't fuck with you; we only fuck with da Zoo!"

Just like that, we had won the race. I removed my helmet to a cheering crowd. I was sweating and my breathing was rapid. I squinted my eyes to clear my vision. When I spotted Bookstore Girl standing there. The leader of Blaze N' Fire came up to me. I pointed to her. "Go pay the lady," I told him.

When he walked off, the guys came up to me. Foe jumped up and down in the air. "Yo that was some crazy shit!"

I could see Preach watching me. "You ain't never did no shit like that before," Diamond said excitedly.

Zu then came up, "A hunnid bands and we're not going to see a dime of it are we? Who is she?"

"Someone that needed help."

Zu nodded. "Always been someone's savior."

"I got y'all though. Come to my house tomorrow we need to talk," I told him.

Zu walked off, back to the group. Meanwhile, I needed to get out of here.

I hopped on my bike and dipped off.

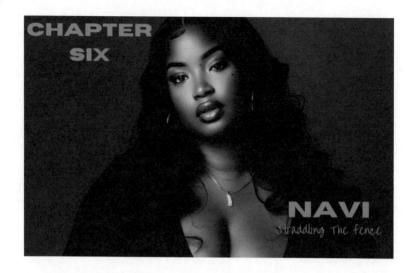

CHAPTER SIX

NAVI

Straddling The Fence

I stepped into the precinct with all eyes on me. When Preach left my house after the shit with Jackson, I had to make it look like self-defensive. It kind of was. I had to hand over my gun and badge until the internal affairs bureau gave me approval. I saw my father standing in my lieutenant's office talking to him. My stomach sunk. I didn't know what they were in there talking about, but I could only imagine. Although he was retired, somehow, he was still a part of something.

I waited outside the door for him to come out. When he did, my father glared at me coldly as my lieutenant stood between the frame of the door, holding his hand out. I handed over my gun and badge.

"Once they clear you then you will get it back. Until then take some time off."

"What about the case? I'm undercover and I know I can get him to talk. I just need more time."

"Navi, you're off the case. We have to find a different approach. You cannot go near them. If you do, you don't have to worry about this gun and badge anymore."

A part of me was sad about it, but a larger part of me was happy. I needed this break. The only part that scared me was Preach, which meant I needed to give him up and I was in way too deep to do that.

I knew they would need time to strategize a new plan, so it was enough time to tell Preach he really needed to step away from his friends for a while. We had built the case around June 'Chevy' Calloway, so if Preach wasn't involved in anything else, I could keep him safe. I damn near skipped out of the precinct after turning my stuff in. I knew when it was time to face internal affairs I needed to cease all happiness.

As I walked out, the sound of my father's voice caught my attention, making my body still. "Did you do it on purpose?"

The saliva in my mouth dried up immediately. My palms begin to sweat. I was afraid to look him in the eye because him asking me a question wasn't that simple. He was ready to interrogate me. My father prided himself on keeping his and his family name clear of any mess.

I responded to him without looking at him. "No, he was trying to assault me."

"Navanna look at me."

I closed my eyes tightly before turning around. When I did, I opened them, giving him a straight face. *Game on.* Yes, daddy was good at getting people to crack, but the one thing he forgot was he taught me well. "Daddy, you know me better than that. Jackson was a creep who prayed on me everyday I walked into this building. When he assaulted me, I let his ass have it."

He stepped back, watching me. "You really like this young man, don't you?"

"Wha- what are you talking about."

"I wasn't born yesterday. I worked in this same precinct for over thirty years. I still know what goes on. You put your job on the line for this man. It's obvious you like him. I raised you better than this. You mixed business with pleasure," He grilled me.

I didn't know what to say because he was right. Preach had become someone I liked a lot. I knew he wasn't a bad person. He was struggling with making the right decision, just as I was. My father's eyes bored into mine. "Bring him to dinner this Saturday," he said as he walked off.

I exhaled deeply. I didn't even know if Preach would do it. Something so simple as to take down one person turned into this. Preach and I needed to have a talk, and I hoped he was going to be on board because all of this was to save him.

It had been a few days since I'd seen Pretty. I became curious why she hadn't called or texted. I called up Diamond to do me a solid. He was taking forever to pull up. Right as I was about to call him, I saw his bike coming up the street. He pulled up alongside my car, revving his bike and making noise. He lifted his visor, laughing.

"Nigga stop playing!" I shouted.

He parked his bike and hopped off. I got out of the car with a special bouquet of lilies I had made for Pretty. I wanted to show my appreciation to her for not calling the laws on me and my boys. It was a tremendous risk, and she did that shit for me. Pretty was the woman for me. I felt it in my spirit. I wanted her to be mine, so if it meant I had to court her first, so be it. Along with that, I wanted to take her away from here for a while, so I also purchased tickets to leave the country. I wanted it to be just me and her. I knew it was probably a lot trying to juggle me and the job I figured with this time away, it would allow us both to clear our heads.

Diamond and I stepped up to her door. Before knocking, I glanced over at Diamond, who was shaking his head. "You sure you want to do this corny shit?"

"Just because you don't have game don't mean I don't. Just do what I asked, nigga."

I tapped on the door, waiting for her to answer.

"Nigga, I sing but this is a little old let me sing some Ginuwine or something. Man, this shit is—"

The door opened and Diamond quickly turned and began crooning. *"Darling yooou-ah-oo send me,"* he snapped while singing at the same time.

Pretty began smiling, then blushing. The door opened wider, and two more girls appeared. Their eyes brightened as Diamond continued to sing. I handed Pretty the flowers. The more she smiled, the more I knew she was the one. Seeing her, I knew she was going to be my wife. God put it in my heart.

I looked over at Diamond who I figured would have stopped singing by now, but his eyes were closed, his head was back. He was going to town with this song.

"Whoa-ah-ah-oo- you-ah-oo send me."

I gritted my teeth, "Nigga you can stop."

He just kept going until I backhand his arm. "Oh shit, my bad." He smiled.

I leaned over toward him. "But it's corny shit, right?" I turned my attention back to Pretty. I nodded at her, "Who are these ladies?"

She smiled, looking back at them. "These are my sisters. This is Rayana and this is Zaria," she pointed at them.

They all resembled each other, beautiful, brown-skinned women. Diamond leaned in, cheesing hard as hell. "I'm Diamond," he said to them.

I saw one of her sisters drooling over Diamond. "I came by Pretty because I wanted you to know I appreciate you so much. I want you to be my girlfriend. Can I have you Pretty?"

She swung from side to side like a schoolgirl. "Yes!" she smiled giddily.

I leaned forward expecting to be respectable in front of her family giving her a peck but, Pretty was on a different type of time as she kissed me nastily. I was ready to take her thick ass to the back to give her some more of this unholy dick, but I kept it cool.

She handed her flowers to her sister while Zaria stared at Diamond. She wasn't looking at his face, instead; she peered at his jacket. I ignored it because she wasn't my focus. Pretty was.

"I will pick you up later to take you out so be ready. I have another surprise for you."

Diamond and I went to walk off, but she grabbed my wrist. "Wait. Umm we're having dinner at my parents Saturday I want you to come," she asked.

Meeting a woman's parents was something I had never experienced before, but because I was really into her, I was cool with it, if that's what she wanted. "Ok. I got you Pretty. Go enjoy the time with your sisters, I'll see you later."

Diamond and I continued back to our rides. "Oh, nigga you fucked her. Aye, I need her sister, you see how she was looking at me. I know when someone wants me."

"Hook yourself up."

Diamond hopped on his bike, taking off. Me, there were some loose ends I needed to tie. The drive took me about twenty minutes to get where I needed to be. I parked once I arrived, got out, and walked up to the front door. I knocked a few times and waited.

The door opened to Simone, looking sick that I had just showed up. "You gone let a nigga in or make me stand outside."

She hesitantly let me in. The house was dark. The air was thick, and tension filled the space we were in. "Why are you here?" she muttered.

"I came to talk."

She crossed her arms over her chest, "You still with the Cop?"

So, she knew as well. "How you know?"

"Because I do. Now, I asked you a question!" she snapped.

My head flew back. I waved my hand in front of her. "Simone watch how you talk to me. If I was, it has nothing to do with you."

Simone had a jealous filled heart. You could smell the shit from a mile away. She was beautiful, yes, but it had always been something about her that never seemed right since the day she walked in the church. I even tried tilting my head to the side, squinting my eyes to see if maybe I was the one who was tripping, but I wasn't. My heart knew exactly who it wanted, and it wasn't Simone.

"She played you. She's an angel in disguise and you're still fucking with her. But me," she pointed to herself. "I tried apologizing and you threw me away like trash. So, what the fuck makes her so special?"

She had a point, but Pretty showed me I could trust her Simone, she didn't. Pretty made me feel something Simone didn't. Pretty's pussy was handcrafted for me, Simone's wasn't.

"Right, can't say shit. I hope you and those sorry ass niggas go back to jail."

I took a step back. "Hold on, you talking spicy. Simone you were just crying crocodile tears. You lucky we let yo ass go!" I shouted.

"Well, I had a revelation," she hissed. "Does your daddy know you out there killing people? Does he know his son who comes into the house of God every Sunday faithfully is committing crimes as soon as he steps his raggedy ass feet over that threshold? I should tell your fa—"

My hands went around her neck. I began squeezing. Simone's hands clung onto mine. She tried pulling my hands off, but my grip around her neck became tighter. She scratched and clawed at me. *Tighter.* I gritted my teeth as I stared her in her eyes. "A fucking demon. A jezebel. A serpent." I mumbled as I shook her.

Tighter. Who was she to tell me my truth? I didn't like her ass. *Tighter.* I was mad at myself for showing up, for getting involved with her to begin with. *Tighter.* It seems the more I stray away from church; the Devil finds a way to use me. Simone's eyes fluttered while she tried to sip in air. *Tighter.*

"I pray God places peace in your heart. I pray you get everything you deserve. I-I," I released her.

Simone dropped to the floor, gasping for air. I couldn't do it. I didn't bother to say anything else. I just prayed she would walk away from the situation as I have.

"When did you get a boyfriend Navi?" I asked after the guys left.

Navi smiled from ear to ear. Happy, giddy, schoolgirl like. It was nice to see her this way. She sniffed the fresh flowers he had given her while Rayana and I stared.

"It wasn't supposed to happen, but it did," she said, now turning to us.

"Ooo was the dick good? You know they say the skinny niggas be packing," Rayana chimed in.

A soft giggle came from Navi. *That man was dicking her down.* I was less interested in what went on in the bedroom and more interested in how she connected with him. When I saw the other guy wearing that jacket, I wanted to ask so many questions. Like about the man who fucking saved my life and somehow put extra money in my pocket. I honestly just wanted to find him to tell him thank you.

Navi plopped down on the couch, "He's going to meet daddy."

My eyes grew wide. Now I knew for sure the bitch tripped on the dick and fell in love. I hadn't even brought Cortez around my daddy. He wasn't even a pinch of what our father expected us to bring around. Seeing them, especially a biker crew, Navi had to be in a cloud. Rayana burst into laughter. "You are tripping. Daddy will not buy anything that nigga is selling, but I see you girl," she said, shaking her head from side to side.

I jumped right in. "How did you meet him?"

Her eyes steered away. "My case."

Rayana gasped loudly, falling back on the couch. "Oh, yeah bitch you're tripping."

"It just happened. I like him a lot," she mumbled.

I leaned forward tapping her leg, "Well if you like him, we love him."

"I want his friend. He's fine." Rayana jumped in.

I rolled my eyes. "That nigga looks toxic."

"I'm a nurse I'll just give myself an IV if I overdose on his toxicity." She winked.

We all burst out laughing. I glanced at Navi, clearing my throat. I really wanted to ask how I could find the Zoo Boyz, but decided against it because I didn't need her knowing how I was searching for a man. It sounded desperate. However, I wanted Cortez's ass gone and my money he stole. I wasn't about to forget he had taken almost thirty grand out of my account.

"Navi, I need a favor," I asked.

Both of their eyes surveyed me, making me feel small. I'd never asked for any favors from either of them, including my parents. "What is it?"

I took a deep breath, "I want to rob Cortez and—"

"What the fuck! Why?"

Rayana scooted to the edge of the couch. "I got to hear this," she said.

I rubbed my palms together because I felt like my nerves were getting the best of me. "He cheated on me. He stole from me. I want my shit back. Once I get what I need I'm going to go away for a while."

"Wait, what about your store and who wants his broke ass?" Navi said.

I cut my eyes at her.

Navi shrugged her shoulders. "What? Now you know I was going to find out if the nigga had money. It's ok Zari we learn from our mistakes. But I can't help you rob anybody."

The nerve, but she was out her fucking on a nigga who's a whole criminal. "Are you serious? Fine I will do it myself." I shot up from the couch.

Rayana grabbed my wrist. "Wait a damn minute. Now I'm all for slashing fucking tires. Bleaching clothes, but you're talking about committing a felony. What do you want us to do?"

"I want you bitches to have my back. For once have my fucking back!" I shouted.

I went to leave, but I wanted to remind them of something. "Navi let's not forget who helped you make detective and Rayana if it wasn't for my connections your ass wouldn't be working in that fucking hospital," I finished as I left her house.

I know my ask was extreme, but there wasn't another option. I tried doing it the right way, now it was going to be my way. I wanted him to pay, regardless if he had it or not.

"Mm, baby," I moaned.

Preach's tongue traveled through each one of my toes. He sucked on them like he was a foot connoisseur. His hand caressed my thighs, gripping them tightly, then stroking them softly. His tongue traveled up my legs, giving me all the feels. I love how he appreciates every part of my body. He never made me feel uncomfortable when I was naked. I would normally be shy, but with him I was comfortable.

The way his hands touched me shot a tingle through my body. I felt like I was on a cloud, and I didn't want to come down.

"Damn Pretty, pussy wetter than a slip and slide," he growled.

Preach stood sitting in the chair across from me, he held his dick in his hands waving it back and forth. "Come ride it."

The skinny niggas have big dicks wasn't a myth. He was packing. I love it. I got up, strutting over to him. I eased on top, riding the wave. "Mm, I want more and more," I moaned.

I couldn't get enough of it. Preach had completely sucked me in. Not just the sex, but how he was a gentleman, a protector, and a man of God. He was a lot of Holy and a little hood.

Up, then down, roll my hips.

"That's right Pretty work those hips. Shit feels so so good," he moaned as his head fell back.

Up, then down, roll my hips.

I was in bliss, in love, and I knew it. He knew how to make me feel like I was the only woman who existed in his life. It was a feeling I cherished.

I bit into my bottom lip, closing my eyes and letting go. Preach gripped my ass cheeks, spreading them wide, picking me up, then lying me on the floor. "Let's get real nasty, Pretty."

He ran his dick up and down my slit. When he went back inside, he rolled his hips so good my eyes shot open. He then stuck two fingers in my mouth, and I sucked on them like it was dick.

"Oh Preach!"

"Prentice Pretty you can say Prentice."

He took his hand out of my mouth, place one leg over his shoulders and the other he spread wide. When I glanced up, I could see the spit fall from his mouth and felt it hit my clit as he began rubbing on it and I lost it. I wanted to say God, but I wasn't about to fuck up this session. "Damn daddy!" I called out.

"*Fuck!*" he grunted.

"Oo I-I,"

I wanted to tell him I loved him. Maybe it was the sex, but now it's what I felt.

"I know you do Pretty, I know."

"I love you, Prentice!" I screamed.

He and I rocked for the next hour until we exploded together. We didn't even move, he and I laid on the floor cuddling. He didn't tell me he loved me back, making me feel stupid. I felt his lips on my ear, "I love you too Pretty. I do."

He stroked my face so gently. I backed up further on him, snuggling in his embrace. "How do you know you love me?" I asked.

"I'm a man that knows exactly what he wants. I knew I loved you since the day I followed you to my father's church. I stand on that Pretty."

A smirk eased onto my face then disappeared because it was time for me to tell him he couldn't be with his friends. He had to stay away, otherwise he was going to end up meeting his demise.

I turned my head, glancing at him.

"What's up? What's on your mind?" he asked.

It was as if he could read my mind. "Do you think you'll ever give up what you're doing to be what your father wants you to be?"

"I think about it all the time. I believe God is trying to reach me, but I've always been a stubborn man."

I nodded. "Do you want to be in the church full time? Maybe mentor the youth. Help kids that kind of live like you?" I asked.

"I thought about it."

I now turned fully his way. "Maybe you need to really pray about it. I prayed for a man like you and you're here."

He laughed, "You said you don't believe in God."

"I believe in a higher power, not sure what it is or who it is, but someone heard it."

He tapped my nose. "It was God Pretty."

"I think you should step away from Zoo for a while. Especially while this case is still on going. I—"

His head flew back. "Fuck is you talking about?" he paused now sitting up. "Those niggas are my brothers there is no leaving Zoo, I am Zoo!" he shouted.

"Preach, baby, listen to me. I know the outcome of this. If you do not step away, you're going to go down with Chevy and I don't want that for you," I tried explaining. "I love you, I want to be with you and if you're tied into that it means I can lose you."

He shook his head. "So, what you want a nigga to choose? Huh?" he said, now getting up and putting his clothes on.

I didn't want things to go like this. "Preach wait."

"No, those niggas are the reason I'm alive. Everybody want a nigga to go be in church, but nobody knows the same nigga behind that pulpit is the same nigga that left me on the streets. The same nigga that won't accept his own blood. Talking about leave Zoo. If it's my fate to go down with my brothers, then that's what it is. When you choose me, you choose Zoo, but it's clear you're not for me. That trip, let's press pause for a while," he finished.

I was speechless. I didn't want him to leave. I could feel the tears welling in my eyes. "Preach I—"

"Nah Pretty, this isn't going to work." He said, walking out of my house and slamming the door.

I couldn't believe this shit. My phone rang. I didn't even want to answer it, but I did. "Hello?"

"Detective Richardson, you're back on the case. Be in the office tomorrow at eight am."

Shit!

CHAPTER SEVEN

CHEVY

Accepting Fate

I left the building, walking toward my car. I folded the piece of paper up, putting it in my pocket. When I reached my car, I dropped my head. I flicked my nose, then pinched the bridge of it. *I don't have time for this shit today.* Lola was leaning against my shit with her arms crossed over her chest. The smirk she held only agitated me.

I tried ignoring her, going to the driver's side to get in. "You can't ignore me. You know."

I halted as my eyes landed on hers while she rocked her head from side to side. "Yes, I can."

"What do you want from me? You know I've never met a woman as desperate as you."

"I want some dick. One time and I will leave you alone, I promise."

Something told me she had her fingers crossed behind her back. "You can't handle it," I told her.

"You don't know that."

The way she was acting was the main reason for me not fucking her. "No!"

"Then I'm telling Harvey and before you say she already knows, I know you're lying."

It was the extorting tactic that bothered me. "Lola Sanchez, is it? You really don't want to play this game with me. Does daddy know his little spoiled fucking brat is out here trying to extort people? Does he know that his daughter out here fucking any and every nigga that has a little money in their pockets. Pussy so loose can't even wrap around a dick. Lola, go find another sucker-ass nigga because I'm not it. If you want to tell Harvey fine. But fucking you is not an option," I said as I got in my car, speeding off.

I hit the steering wheel over and over. *Fuck!* I know I had given Harvey two months, but that shit was about to be cut in half. Karma was catching up to me and my time was running out. I didn't know if I wanted to pull up on her and have this conversation or go home and pack my shit and ride out. I glanced at my phone, debating if I was going to call her or not.

I snatched the phone up, unlocking it only for my mother's number to be the first to appear.

I quickly got over, pulling up to the first curb I spotted. I stared at the number as I held my phone in my hand. I tried doing this before but couldn't go through with it. Something about this moment put fear in me. I hit the number to dial out. I placed it to my ear as it rung. *What if she doesn't want to see you? What if she never answers? What will I say?* My thoughts were going so fast, I didn't realize someone had picked up the line.

"This is Grace," her voice sounded like a mother.

She sounds like a suburban housewife. I wanted to scream Mommy, but I couldn't. I opened my mouth slightly, but nothing came out.

"Hello? Who is this?"

I hung up. I couldn't do it. My pride was too big to allow me to. "*Fuck, fuck, fuck!*" I shouted.

I took a deep breath as I started the car up. When I glanced over, I realized I was in front of Bookstore Girl's shop. Although it was open, I noticed it had a for sale sign on the window. I took note as I drove off.

It was time to close the loop up on some things. First start was Zu. I pulled up to the Orange Village, where I knew I could find him. Oddly, he was the only nigga here. I got out walking inside. "Zeus!" I called out.

Zu came from the back with a curiosity on his face. "Chevy, what's up?"

Zu and I had it out so many times, but we addressed none of our issues. We chucked it up and moved like he and I had never argued. We had come to this after over ten years of friendship. "Let's roll up first," I told him.

I needed him to be chill while we talked. Zu tends to get defensive when he's in the wrong, and the goal was for us to hash shit out. I didn't want this situation to blow up more than it should have. Zu rolled us a blunt. We began smoking. I gave it a little time for it to kick in before I started. Zu leaned back on the bar.

"Why are you here?" he asked.

I flicked my nose. "Zu, nigga you know why I'm here. What's up? Why would you put my business up? What kind of trouble are you in? huh?"

He took another puff of the blunt and began choking, handing it to me. "Damn nigga you gone ask all the questions or let me answer?" he started. "I was in a bind. I knew we was going to win. I-I—"

I waved my hand. "Hold the fuck up. What if we would have lost? That's the problem my nigga," I pointed to the side of my head. "You don't use your fucking brain. Nigga you got to grow up!" I barked.

Zu had now stood, but I wasn't done. I clapped my hands together. "You talk about me being in charge of everything. Look at the decisions you're making. How can I trust that you will make sure the crew is good if you're out here making fucked up decisions? Zu, my nigga this isn't the first time. This is why I can't fucking trust you," I gritted. "It's all about Zeus! Nigga you're not a God. Yo daddy should have named you something else."

Zu rushed over to me, so I stood. "Watch yo mouth Chevy because for real the next move is going to be my best move."

I pinched my lips together and nodded. "What about Harvey? Huh? I told you everything you needed to know, but you listened to nothing I fucking said. You better tighten up before she be off with the next nigga, one that will treat her like she's a queen. Kissing her feet every fucking night. Making sure her belly is full and she is fucked real good."

I could see his jaws tighten. "You said you never fucked her."

I shook my head. "This is how I know you got too much shit going on. It's not me you got to worry about," I pointed to his chest. "What about Dio? Your fucking blood out here running theses streets reckless. You're supposed to be guiding him but the little nigga hanging in the projects, but who am I? I see we're not going to get nowhere. Nigga you need to wake up."

I could hear him chuckle. "Mr. Know It All. Ok, I fucked up and I apologize but you want a nigga to beg. I'm not doing that Chev. I—"

"I want you to grow up! We supposed to be kings out this muhfucka, but you are not a king you a fucking joker. Zu be easy my nigga."

With that, I left. I didn't know if Zu and I would fix our friendship, but I hoped we did before my departure. If not, I was accepting our fate as ex- best friends.

Navi had been blowing my phone up since leaving her house that day. I needed time away from her. I could feel the burden of the storm God was creating on my shoulders. If I say I didn't love her, it would be a lie, but making me choose was not an option. I felt trapped in the same position my father put me in, making me choose between the streets and the church.

I felt like nobody understood me. Today was not only Diamond's birthday, but also the day I was to go meet Navi's parents. Although I was mad at her, I was still a man of my word. I kneeled at the altar, placing my hands together. I needed to ask God for guidance. I needed direction because the way I was moving was taking a toll on me.

"You still pray when you're lost and confused?" my father's voice made me lift my head.

"I never stop praying even when things are good in my life. I always give glory to God," I said as I stood now facing him.

He sat on the pew in front of me. His eyes weren't one of a parent in this moment, yet of someone who was judging me. A feeling came over me, making me feel like a child standing before him. Me staring at my father; I was waiting for him to say that he loved me. That he accepted me even though I had flaws, but I knew deep down he wouldn't do it.

"If you have all this love you say for God, why can't you give him all of you? He's waiting."

I didn't have an answer. "I-I—"

He held his hand up. "Prentice it's in you. You're not missing out on nothing, but trouble doing whatever it is you are out there. Let's not forget you got arrested for hanging with them hood Negros."

"How can you sit there and tell me about the choices I've made when you." I pointed at him. "My father shut me out. Have you asked God for forgiveness? Have you!" I raised my voice.

My father's head tilted to the side. He knew exactly what I was talking about. He gave up on me. He put me out and expected me to still follow behind him. He had no clue what I experienced out on those streets. He stood coming toward me, "Prentice I—"

"No, you have no idea what pushing me away did. I prayed everyday I was on those streets. I was lost and I still prayed. I came to you, begged you and you turned your back on me. What would God say? You know Diamond's grandmother took me in. The same guy you frown upon helped me," I said, slapping my hand against my chest.

I could feel the tears building up. I didn't want to get emotional, but this between him and me needed to happen. There was no way I could move forward without telling him how I felt. "He saw me at my worst. Between a crackhead mother and father who loves his church more than his only son. I had nothing to live for. I was going to kill myself the night Diamond came to me offering me shelter. I was going to kill myself even though I knew it was wrong. My friends saved me. Now here it is you standing before me asking me to choose." I wiped my face from the tears that escaped me. "I have family out there and if they need me, I will be there."

His body stilled, shocked by my words. "Prentice I just want what's best for you."

I nodded. "I will preach on the last Sunday of the month. I'm doing it for him," I pointed upward. "I owe to him."

I placed my hand on my father's shoulder. "I love you pops," I said as I walked out of the church.

I pinched the bridge of my nose to clear any tears that tried to escape. I hopped on my bike and took off. I felt free for the first time. I had spoken my truth to a man I feared. I rode until I reached the address Navi gave me for her parent's home. When I arrived, I noticed the neighborhood was a little more than modest. I parked my bike walking up to their door. I didn't have to knock because the door open before I could. Her sister Zaria looked at me and smiled. "Hi."

"Hello, is Navi here I didn't see her car," I said.

She opened the door wider to let me come in. As I stepped inside, I could hear light giggles. She was here. I knew Pretty's laugh anywhere. Zaria walked me over to the living room where Pretty was sitting on the couch looking as beautiful as the day I met her.

"Navi, you have company," her sister told her.

When she turned to see me standing there, a light lit up in her eyes, one that made my heart race. I wish she understood my situation and didn't make me choose. Thinking about how she wanted me to let my niggas go down catching cases for shit I was involved in pissed me off all over again. It only made me want to turn around and leave. She hopped up from the couch, skipping to me. She took my hand into hers, raising only her eyes to me. "Hey baby," she cooed.

Eyes on her. "Don't do that. I'm here because I said I would be," I whispered.

Her demeanor changed, and that was fine because we were not on good terms. Pretty led me into the living room, calling out to her father, "Daddy, I want you to meet someone," she said softly.

He rose from the chair, standing not too much taller than me, slim build with a salt and pepper beard and a fucked up military cut. Just by his stature, I could tell that he was about to be on some stupid shit. He didn't like me. He was judging as soon as he saw me. Her mother greeted me as she came around, standing next to her husband. Her smile was bright like Pretty's. All three of the girls took from their mother.

"It's so nice to meet the son of Dr. Kingston. I've heard your father preach and it's something special." she cheesed.

"Ma, please he doesn't want to talk about church. I'm sorry," Pretty said as she looked at me.

"It's ok, Pretty, I'm used to it. Thank you, ma'am."

Her father sighed. "So y'all got little nicknames and shit. Navanna," he called out.

Before he could say another word, Pretty's mother jumped in, saying dinner was ready. We all went into the dining room to a full spread. I hadn't had a home cook meal in years. Shit, Grandma G used to burn but then she started burning for real. They all went to sit until her mother stopped them. "Can we bless the food. Prentice, would you like to say grace?"

I side eyed Pretty. She looked at me, then pulled her eyes away.

"Sure."

They all bowed their heads as I started prayer. Once finished, we all sat. Her father stared me down for what seemed like minutes until Zaria began speaking, "So you ride bikes?"

I nodded. "Yes, I do."

"I saw your friend's jacket, Zoo Boyz, is it a large crew?"

I took a swig of water. "Small group."

"But where do you work? If you have time to ride bikes, when do you have time to work?" Her father started drilling me with questions.

Pretty's eyes pleaded with him. "Daddy please."

"No!" he shouted.

This shit escalated quickly. I lifted my head and calmly told him, "Don't yell at her."

He placed both elbows on the table while pointing at me. "Don't tell me how to talk to my child. Did you know she risked her career dealing with you? So yes, I want to know what you do. If she were to lose her job, how will she be cared for?"

My eyes bounced on everyone at the table, then back on her father. I was trying to decide if I wanted to remain holy or flip this fucking table and head-butt his ass. It was the assumption that pissed me off more than his tone. I had now leaned forward, looking him in his eyes.

"Sir, Mr. Richardson I am a person of Christ, but I'm a man first so please speak to me with some respect."

A laugh bellowed from him. "You're a criminal, one that uses his bike gang as a ploy. Oh, and all that God shit doesn't work with me."

I nodded. The table had become quiet. Pretty went to speak, but I placed my hand on hers. I went into my pocket, pulling out my wallet. I tossed my business card on the table. "That right there is my business, mine. A million- dollar- a- year business, sir. Legal, legit," I started.

Chevy made us all invest in businesses. He showed us the ins and outs, so even if the illegal ones fell through; we had something to stand on.

I pulled another out of my wallet and tossed it on the table. "Do not judge others, and you will not be judged. For you will be treated as you treat others. Romans chapter fourteen verse one through four."

He stood from the table as his chest heaved in and out. I placed my cards back into my wallet, then in my pocket. I picked up a piece of fried chicken taking a bite. "This is some good chicken, ma'am.

"Nigga, get out of my house. Coming in here trying to show off. Navanna, this is not going to work. Eating my food and shit."

I took another look at him. "Proverbs chapter twenty verse seven. A righteous man walks in integrity. Blessed are his children after him," I said, now standing. "Pretty let's go," I calmly told her.

"My child is not going anywhere."

I smiled. "I didn't want things to go like this, but this is what you chose. Pretty is leaving with me. Now, Mr. Richardson I hope to see you at church tomorrow. We need to hold prayer for you. You have a soul that needs redeeming. Pretty, let's go!" I barked.

"I know this nigga—"

"Let it go!" I heard her mother yell.

I headed for the door, not looking to see if Pretty was behind me. If her ass didn't walk out of this house, it was over. I calmly walked out of the house getting on my bike. I started revving up, and she had yet to step foot out the fucking door. I hit the kickstand, getting ready to back up. Pretty came running out with the biggest smile on her.

"Let's fucking ride!" she screamed.

"Good girl, Pretty," I said as I backed up and sped off.

Preach standing up to my father was something I wasn't expecting. The nice nasty attitude he delivered set my soul on fire. If I could have fucked him right then and there, I would have. The way my father was acting only showed me he has no desire to see me happy. He wanted to choose who we were with, and not who we wanted to be with. It explained why Zaria had never brought Cortez around. It made me a tinge emotional because I love my father and what he thinks, but I was falling in love with Preach and this moment really did it for me.

He sped down the highway with me gripping him tightly. My short babydoll style dress blew with the wind while he dipped in and out of traffic like a madman. My adrenaline was on a thousand. My hands slowly traveled down his stomach, to his pants, unzipping them, and sticking my hand inside. I wanted him to fuck me on this bike. His head turned slightly, but because of the helmet, I couldn't see his face. He went to the hill that overlooked the Hollywood sign. Once we reached the top, he hit his kickstand getting off, but holding his hand out for me to stay on.

Preach removed his helmet, gazing at me. "Pretty I want you to know I'm going to always protect you even if you feel like I shouldn't. That situation back there could have gotten real nasty, but for your sake I walked away. When I dedicate myself to someone, I'm fucking dedicated and there is no changing my mind even if I'm upset at you because that feeling is only temporary."

I understood what he was saying, but right now I wanted him inside me. I chewed on the side of my lip using my index finger, signaling him to come to me. Preach's lips curled into a smile. He strolled my way, nuzzling his face into my neck. "I hope you got balance."

"I got whatever you need," I uttered.

His tongue slid across my neck, up to my lips, taking my them into his mouth. The feeling of freedom coursed through my body. I knew the love that had brewed up in me for Preach was more than I expected. If it meant I had to step away from this case, so be it. I knew he would do whatever it took to take care of me, and I wanted to be by his side as he would be for me.

His hands caressed my thighs as I gripped what I could of his bike. As his fingers tiptoed up my thigh, my legs began spreading wider. He didn't even bother to pull my panties off. He merely moved them to the side, sliding one finger over my clit before allowing his dick to play with my pussy. He brought his finger to his lips, licking the taste of me off it.

He nodded his head, bringing his forehead to mine. "I'm obsessed," I moaned as I rolled my hips to match his pace.

He gripped the back of my neck, yanking it back just slightly, "Don't be obsessed, be in love Pretty, now fuck on this dick."

It was the two sides of Preach that I loved and the more his hood side came out the more I turned into putty. His thumb stroked the side of my face until I captured it with my mouth. I sucked on his thumb as our eyes remained on each other. His arm extended and his hips rolled sending his dick in a wavelike motion.

"Motherfuck!" I screamed.

His eyes lowered as he bit into his lip. "That's right Pretty. Let this dick love you. This sweet pussy feels so good," he grunted.

"Ah! My- my—"

He slowly shook his head. *Don't say it.* He mouthed.

I just bit into my lip, closing my eyes. I felt the tingle emerging. "Ooo," I cried.

"Cum Pretty, cum for me."

Preach went from slow to pounding me out and the cum I released not only covered him but also trickled down the side of his bike. The entire shit was sexy and wild. There was no way I was giving this man up.

He and I rode back until we reached my house. He'd invited me to his friend's birthday party, and I damn sure was showing up. I needed all the bitches to know that he was mine. When I entered my house, it startled me to see not only my father sitting on the couch but my lieutenant. I must have been so wrapped up in Preach I hadn't noticed their cars outside. I didn't know what this was about, but something told me it wasn't good.

CHAPTER EIGHT

CHEVY

A Party To Remember

W hen I pulled up to Diamond's, I noticed the city had come out to celebrate with him for his birthday. I footed the bill. I wanted my boy's thirtieth to be one he would never forget. My takeoff day was approaching and being able to spend these last few weeks with my friends was important. I parked, and got out, making my way into his lounge.

The sound of the music blared as I opened the door to enter. The orange color with a sprinkle of brown was a crazy view against the black lights. I watched as people partied and mingled. I really wanted to open up more to the guys, but watching how happy they were, I just couldn't. Me being a burden in one's life wasn't the plan; I didn't have it in me.

They all wanted to travel with me, but it was a time for solace to connect with myself. At this stage in my life, I was just existing, living for me was taking care of others. Showing them the ropes so they could use what I've taught them toward others.

I spotted Foe strolling up to me. "You straight? You want to talk about it?"

"Always good," I lied.

I was fucked up. I allowed my pride to get the best of me. Foe eyed me curiously. He leaned in, "Want a drink? A blunt?"

I reached in my pocket, pulling out a pre-rolled blunt. I pointed to the dark corner. I walked over to the isolated corner, sitting and watching everyone else. When Diamond appeared from the back, the crowd went crazy. From people taking pictures and recording videos, it was so much love in the room for him. It was like an unofficial red-carpet event.

"We only fuck with the Zoo!" they screamed.

Watching him pop the most expensive champagne as I smoked my blunt was nice. No matter the shit we were in, that could go to shit at any time, these niggas stayed happy. I tried it but it didn't work for me. My eyes fell back on the door when I noticed the girl from the bookstore enter with two other girls. I leaned back in my chair as my eyes followed her through the lounge. She smiled. I'd finally seen her fucking smile, and the shit made a nigga's stomach feel funny.

I placed the blunt back to my lips as I continued to watch her. The sound of Harvey's voice pulled my eyes away, "Chev, why are you all the way back here. Come and have some fun," she whined.

"I'm straight."

She plopped down in the chair in front of me. "Why are you like this? I get it. You're traveling to see your mom, but you can't stop living because of that. I haven't even seen you smile in years."

There was nothing to smile about. "I wish y'all would just fucking stop," I gritted.

Harvey rolled her eyes. "That shit doesn't scare me, but if you want to sit in this corner looking like Eeyore then fine," she said as she stood dancing her way back into the crowd.

My eyes scanned the crowd looking for Bookstore Girl. However, my eyes landed on trouble, big fucking trouble. She slowly strutted up to the table.

"Chevy," she called out.

"Lola."

"I see you still searching for dick?"

A sinister smile eased on her face. She pulled a tiny piece of paper out of her purse. It had a number on, "This better be some digits to a fucking phone number."

She leaned over, pushing her ass out in the air, "Figured I'd give you one more chance before I get to squealing like a canary. You can either pay me what's on that paper or fuck me."

I hated to do it, but I see now I was going to have to. "My house two am," I said to her.

She snatched up the paper, smiling. She said nothing more. She strutted away, shaking that fake ass she carried. I'd never met a woman like her before, and I prayed to God she was the last one I'd come across. I lit my blunt again, trying to enjoy what I could of the party.

Now where did Bookstore Girl go?

Navi convinced Rayana and me to come to a party. My first instinct was to decline until she said it was for the Zoo Boyz. I quickly threw that thought out of my head. After what happen at my parents, her running off with Preach like she was in some fucking movie, I figured she would be in my daddy's face begging for him to forgive her. Navi had shown she was making her own choices. She was choosing love. Me, I was choosing violence. Once we were finished here, I was going to have a meeting with the night.

We could barely get through the tight crowd as we entered the building. I'm happy we got through retrograde because no telling which person was going to act a fool tonight. Rayana began dancing in the tight space we were in while Navi stood on her tippytoes looking for Preach. "I can't see him," she whined.

I rolled my eyes because the dick couldn't be that good for her to be doing all of this. My head bobbed side to side, looking for him, for her. When I spotted him, I tapped her shoulder, pointing. Navi almost tripped over her own two feet flying over to him. Rayana and I followed behind her. As we approached him and Diamond, I could feel Rayana squeeze my hand. Navi tapped Preach's shoulder. It didn't matter who he was talking to. All that shit ceased when he saw my sister. "Pretty you looking good," he said to her, leaning toward her ear saying something that had her cheesing like a fucking Cheshire cat.

Diamond walked around, stepping in front of Rayana, "We meet again, you want a drink? Let a nigga get you something special." He looked at me. "Come on let me take care of y'all," he said, heading toward the bar.

I needed a drink. Navi didn't even look back at us. She stayed where she was; hugged up with Preach. When we reached the bar, Diamond hopped over the bar, ducking down then he popped up. He had two bottles of champagne. He popped them to pour us a glass. I took a sip, then another and another. By the time I glanced down, the glass was empty. I needed all the liquid courage so I could do what I needed after this. Diamond and Rayana had walked off to the dance floor, grinding all on each other.

I took a few more drinks, feeling good as ever. My eyes began searching the crowd for my mystery man. I knew he was a part of the Zoo Boyz, but I didn't see him anywhere. A guy stepped up to me asking me to dance and I accepted. I rocked my hips to the beat. The more I moved my body, the more the liquor was taking over me. I tapped at the front of my thigh as I swiveled my hips low.

My head drifted up slowly. *Eyes on him.* I spotted him. He sat in a dark corner puffing on his blunt. *Eyes on me. Can he see me?* I thought. Then his head nodded up and down as he leaned further back in the chair. A smile crept on my face. He was watching. Dark as midnight, but fine as wine. He wore a tinge of orange and that color against his skin was one you couldn't forget. Our eyes stayed connected.

I continued to move as if I was dancing just for him. *Swivel, tap. Swivel, tap. Swivel, tap.*

I brought myself up and started all over again, still watching him. *Swivel, tap. Swivel, tap.*

Thank you. I mouthed.

Swivel, tap. Swivel, tap.

He held the blunt between his lips as he ran both his hands down the front of his waves. He pulled the blunt from his lips, blowing out smoke. *I got you.* He mouthed back.

THE STREETS & THE PULPIT

It was something about this moment that captured me. I still didn't know his name, but that's what made this so exciting, so exhilarating. The guy behind me placed his hands to my thighs, moving toward my center. I moved his hands away, and he did it again. My eyes landed back on ole boy. He pulled his gun out, setting it on the table, winking. The hands that were on me were now off and the guy had walked away. *Well, damn.* When I glanced back, the mystery man was gone. "Damn!" I spat.

I walked off toward the back and into the ladies' room. Normally when you came to a club of some sort, the bathroom usually had a line, but it was completely empty. I leaned over the sink to wash my hands, trying to prepare my mind for later.

"What's your name?" I heard his voice.

I turned toward him and almost came from how good he looked. "I don't want to tell you," I replied.

"Why?" he stepped closer.

I felt flushed, hot, and turned on.

Closer.

"Why is your name such a fucking secret?"

Closer.

The smell of his cologne captured me, sending my head swinging to catch it. He was now in front of me.

"I wanted to tell you thank you for what you did for me," I mumbled.

"I did it because I wanted to so, no thank you is needed."

I licked my lips, inhaling deeply.

He stepped closer to me, leaning in with his lips grazing my ear just slightly. "Let me ask you something. If I stroked your cheeks softly allowing my eyes to connect with yours, telling you how beautiful you are would you fold or stand on business? I want to know so talk to a nigga nice."

His voice was deep, with a bit of a rasp to it. It gave dominant, prideful, arrogant, and fucking king. He placed his eyes back on mine. The longer he stared, the more intense they became.

"Maybe I'm high or maybe I'm into you; because I know nothing about you, but I want those lips on mine now!" he growled like a hungry animal.

Is my mouth open? "Bu-but we don't know each other," I stuttered.

"And?"

He ran his fingertips around my shoulders, making my body shudder. "*Shit!*" I moaned.

"This is the fourth time we ran into each other. I've never been a man to beg, but for you," he paused. "I will ask again. Let. Me. Taste. Those. Lips."

I was ready to lose my mind and morals if he didn't stop. I clinched onto my stomach. "Uh-uh—"

"Fuck!" someone shouted from outside the door.

He halted, then exited the bathroom. I exhaled deeply. *Fuck Zaria!*

The night was going well. Diamond's party had really turned up. Everybody was drunk or high. Pretty stayed by my side as she indulged in the festivities. I knew she wanted to fuck but my eyes were on alert tonight.

All was good until I spotted Asia come in the building. When she saw Foe, they talked a little and began smoking. Meanwhile, Harvey acted like she wasn't watching them, but I know she was. I wasn't sure where her and Zu stood, but if he saw how her little ass was being private eye, he would fucking snap. I felt Pretty tap my shoulders, so I gave her my attention. "I want you to know I'm stepping away from the case. I backed out. I choose you." She smiled.

I tapped her nose. "I didn't want you to feel you had to choose I would never do that. Whatever happens will happen."

"I know, but I don't want to lose you."

"Pretty, you're going to be my wife. I'm not going anywhere."

I turned back to case the crowd again and Monette was walking in. She looked good as hell, like she'd purposely dressed the way she did to be noticed by Diamond. My eyes scanned for Diamond, who was grinding all on Pretty's sister. I could see Zu and Harvey going back and forth, which caused Foe to jump up, stepping away from Asia. *Ah shit!* Before I could reach them, I heard Monette scream. "This is my nigga!"

"Is that bitch talking to my sister like that?" Pretty snapped.

I couldn't even snatch her up before she hauled off, hitting Monette. "Bitch who you talking to like that!"

Fuck! Pretty and Rayana were both fighting Monette. I guess Monette and Asia formed a bond because she came to help. Shit was getting out of control. Diamond tried stepping in, but the way they were thumping, he would have gotten his ass beat. I clung onto Pretty, pulling her away. "Yo chill the fuck out!" I shouted.

She was so hyped her chest bounced up and down. I saw Chevy coming from the back. Monette's time was up after this. Foe grabbed Asia, swinging her little ass to a corner. The DJ cut the music. Everyone stared at Chevy. "Fuck is going on in here. Huh?" Chevy barked. "I didn't pay for a party so bitches can come and fuck it up." His eyes landed on Monette.

He pinched the bridge of his nose. "Why are you even here?" he calmly asked.

Her eyes landed on Diamond, then back on Chevy. Whatever Diamond planted in her, it was stuck, and she couldn't shake it. Tears welled up in her eyes, "I-I—"

"Nah, Mo you fucked that up," Diamond told her.

"Where the party at!" Dio came through the door with his friends.

Zu almost broke his neck. He had no control over his brother, and that was a huge problem. Zu had been so focused on the crew, Harvey, and whatever he was doing on the side, that Dio was out here wild in these streets. When he tried to control him, that shit went in one ear and out the other with Dio.

"Nigga get yo ass out of here," Zu gritted.

"Ah Zeus, nigga chill—"

The sound of Diamond yelling caught my attention. "What! Where?" his glassy eyes glanced at us as the phone fell out of his hand.

We all stared at him as he looked like he saw a ghost. "What's up nigga?" I asked.

Diamond hauled ass out the door with us behind him. "What is it?" Chevy asked him.

He looked at us. It was the first time I'd ever seen Diamond cry. "My fucking granny man. I-I need to get to the hospital."

"Can you ride?" Chevy asked Diamond.

The nigga was losing it as he paced back and forth. "Can you fucking ride!" he repeated.

Diamond nodded his head up and down. We all knew how he felt about Grandma G. Pretty came up to me. I would have to hold off on what she wanted to do tonight.

"I'll call you later my brother needs me," I told her, kissing her forehead.

Harvey came out of the building. "I'll take care of things here."

"Let's ride!" I heard Chevy.

All five of us hopped on our bikes, taking off to the hospital for Grandma G. I was praying hard as hell that she would pull through whatever happened. If not, Diamond would be no good. The thought of losing a loved one did something to me, making me want to do the one thing I hadn't done since I walked away from her that night.

I needed to go see my mother.

The black tights and hoodie I changed into were so tight on my body. I almost felt like I couldn't breathe. I slid the mask down on my face. I've seen this so many times in movies, I felt like it should be easy. I took a deep breath before getting out of the car. It caught me off guard that the block was completely empty. The neighborhood Cortez lived in kept guys posted everywhere, but tonight, no one was around. I crept up the street until I reach his house. A house that I fucking paid for. *Bitch ass nigga.*

As I thought about all the things I poured into Cortez; my stomach turned. All the sage-burning crystals I carried for healing and protection did nothing for his demonic ass. "Ugh!"

THE STREETS & THE PULPIT

When I reached the side window, I tried glancing around to see if I could see anything, but I saw nothing but darkness. I picked at the flimsy screen, pulling it out. I knew I should have told mystery man he would have helped me because what I was doing was dangerous. I wished my sisters accepted my offer. However, here I was alone. Once the screen was out, I pulled myself up, climbing through the window. I remember Cortez having a small safe in his room, and that was the first place I was going. The house smelled of weed. *Damn, he's here. Please God, let me get through this and I won't do nothing else, I promise.*

Getting on my knees, I began crawling toward the back. The closer I got to the room; I realized what he was doing. He had a bitch in here. *Fuck nigga!* I kept moving until I reached the room. Cortez had his feet planted on the floor spread wide as his body rocked back and forth. The girl's moans were exaggerated. I knew he wasn't fucking her that good. I continue to crawl inside the room. He had backed up, almost stepping on me.

I knew I should have turned around, but I was so close to the fucking safe. I crawled faster to the other side. I was so close to the closet when the lights came on and my head went flying back.

"Who the fuck you think you are sneaking into my shit!" he gritted.

"*Ah!*" I screamed.

Cortez released me, sending me slamming down against the floor. The girl's scream clearly annoyed him. "Shut the fuck up!" he pointed at her.

I tried standing, but he stepped on my leg, dick swing in my face. I almost gagged. "Cortez please. All I want is my money," I cried.

"Zaria?" he called out.

"Yes, yes it's me Cortez please," I pleaded.

He squatted down, pulling the mask up. He began laughing in my face. "You're a silly bitch. Call the police!" he shouted.

I thought he would hit me or even send me flying out of a window, but the nigga said call the police. I panicked. I couldn't go to jail. I rushed over to him, "Cortez please don't!"

A smiled eased on his face. I lifted from the floor and my eyes landed on the young girl he was with. I wanted to tell her ass to run, but she was keeping him away from me.

"Hey!" he clapped his hand.

My head eased back his way.

"I was told you got a hundred grand that didn't belong to you."

"It didn't happen like you think I—"

"I want all of it. None of it belongs to you."

"Fuck you! You took money from me, and you think I'm going to pay you?"

He shrugged his shoulders. "Then I'll call the police. I mean what would your daddy say? You could never use that degree. Burglary is a felony."

I dropped my head in defeat. Then raised my head to look at him. "Fine call the fucking police, because I'm not giving you shit!"

I wanted to call his bluff because I knew him. The money was more important. Cortez had nothing. Honestly, I'd stopped helping him with the rent for this place, so it was only a matter of time before they were putting his ass out. He and I stood there facing each other. Although I held a big girl's face, my stomach was turning inside.

Hours had passed, and I still hadn't heard a word from Preach. I was worried about his friend and him. Rayana worked at the hospital they'd went to. It was now morning. I didn't get an inch of sleep because I had been waiting all night to hear from someone. My phone vibrated, but it wasn't from Preach or Rayana. It was from my lieutenant.

The day I came home to him and my father sitting on my couch like they paid the bills, they wanted me to give up the information I'd collected on the Zoo Boyz. I'd found out that Triece Givens and her brothers were all found dead in their homes. Although they were saying it was a robbery gone bad, my father and lieutenant felt like it had something to do with the Zoo Boyz. They were mostly right, but I wasn't giving any additional information about them.

Right then, I stepped away. I told them I didn't have time to gather too much information on them, which was true because I'd been so wrapped up in Preach. They threatened me with desk duty. I took it completely, removing myself from the case. I had been trying to figure out a way to keep them all safe. The way Preach spoke about the boys; I knew he loved them, and I didn't want to be a part of taking them down.

I hesitantly answered the phone. "Hello," I whispered.

"Detective, you need to get down here now. They arrested your sister."

My heart raced. *My sister?* It had to be Zaria. I hope she didn't do what I think she did. "I'm on my way!"

I hopped out of bed, put on clothes, and rushed out the door. I sped like a bat out of hell to get to the precinct. When I arrived and entered the building, I couldn't even get in all the way before I spotted my lieutenant directing me to follow him down the hall. "She has some serious charges against her. It seems like she was trying to commit burglary. Breaking and entering," he started.

Goddamnit Zaria.

He stopped in front of one of the interview rooms. "This can look bad on your father's name. I can make all this go away for her," he raised his brow.

My stomach sank because I had a feeling of where this was headed. All because she wanted revenge on a nigga that didn't give a fuck about her. "Let me talk to her, please."

He nodded, walking away from me. I opened the door to her in all black with her head between her arms. "Get yo ass up!" I shouted.

Her groggy moans annoyed me. *Was this bitch asleep?* "What did you do?" I asked, sitting across from her.

She brushed her hair out of her face as she sat up. "I wanted my money back. Fuck Cortez!" she spat.

"So, you break into his house? Zaria do you know the situation you put me in, do you?"

She pulled her eyes away from me. "I'm sorry. I didn't think he would really call the police," she mumbled.

I slammed my hand on the table, causing her to jump. "Well, the nigga did. Now look at you. Shit!" I hissed.

She really had no clue what she had done. I clearly had no clue what my sister was going through. It seemed we had made assumptions on each other, thinking one's life was in order, but here we were finding out otherwise. I dropped my head because everything I've done was for nothing. I felt her hand on mine. "I will take my charges and the consequences that comes with it," she said as she stroked my hand.

I knew I couldn't leave my sister in here. What type of person would I be if I did that? I loved her and I knew I only had one option. I stood from the table, walking out of the door. My lieutenant was waiting for me as soon as I exited. I said nothing. I just followed him down the hall.

Right now, was the time I needed God and bad.

We had been sitting in the waiting room for hours. Diamond paced the floor the entire time. I placed my elbow to my knee as my chin rested on my hand. "I think we should pray," I told them.

Silence filled the space. Diamond came over to me holding out his hand, "Yes, let's do that because if my granny doesn't pull through I-I'm going to lose my shit."

I stood, holding my hand out. They all stared, but slowly stood, linking our hands together. Chevy sat there looking at us. I could tell he was harboring things and probably needed this prayer more than any of us. He reluctantly stood, taking Zu and Foe's hands. "Bow y'all head," I told them.

Once they bowed, I began praying. Letting God know his will shall be done. We know he has the last say-so, but Grandma G was a fighter, and Diamond needed her more than anything. I prayed for peace. I prayed for healing. I prayed to strip pride from those who had a wall up. I prayed so hard Diamond began sobbing. "Amen," I said as I embraced him into a hug. "I love you, man, she's going to be alright. You have to believe it," I whispered in his ear.

Two nurses had come out. One we didn't know, the other was Pretty's sister. Diamond glanced at me. I shrugged. He walked over to them, and they lead him to the back. I walked back over, sitting next to Chevy, "You can't let your pride scare you out of receiving love. Not just from us, anyone for that matter. I really don't know what's going on with you but I'm praying for you every day," I whispered to him.

He flicked his nose, shifting his body in another direction. I placed my hand to his knee as I got up. I moved near Foe. "Let me holla at you for a minute."

"Bet."

We both walked out of the hospital away from Chevy and Zu. "What's up with you and Harvey?" I asked.

I was waiting for him to react, but he didn't. When Foe acted bull headed like Chevy, it irritated me. "I told you she's cool people."

"Dog, I saw her in your room that night. What was that about?"

His face tightened up. "You spying on me like some bitch!" he snapped.

I shook my head. "It's not even like that. I'm asking because I see the way you look at her. I know you like her but, she's fucking with Zu."

He dropped his head. "I swear nothing happened. She wanted to talk so, I brought her back to the crib. We're just friends. I do not like her."

Foe was lying. A hard head makes a soft ass. I knew he was going to find out the hard way. I told him I would be back to check on Diamond. I had some place to be. When I left the hospital, I went directly to the place, I could find my mother. She never strayed away too far from the place she loved, which was the home we all once shared.

I circled the block a few times, but I didn't see her. I'd checked a few alleys, even the one I'd last seen her in. I wondered had she succumbed to the streets, and the feeling made me sick. I hadn't forgiven her; I didn't tell her I loved her. There were so many things wrong with this situation that bothered me.

I rode further up the street to see two women, one pushing a basket full of shit while the other walked alongside her looking like she was counting change. It was her. Her appearance had gotten worse since last seeing her. It almost broke me. I sped up on to the curb, stopping my bike right in front of them causing them to jump, then stop. I removed my helmet, staring at my mother. Her teeth were now gummy as she exposed them when she smiled. "Prentice. This my baby isn't he so handsome," my mother tapped her friend's shoulder.

"Can I talk to you?" I asked.

She puffed out her chest, swinging her arms from side to side as she strolled up to me. She went to touch my face, but I moved my head back. "I wanted to tell you I'm preaching next Sunday. You should come. Let me help you," I told.

Her eyes widened, then lowered as she began counting the change in her hand. "Shoot, I-I need a dollar," she mumbled.

"Ma!" I shouted.

"Ten, twenty, sixty. Yeah, because I said it to." She mumbled.

I slapped her hand, knocking the change out of her hand. "I came to tell you I love you and I want you to get better, but you can't even look at me. Your son, me, I'm preaching something you've always wanted to see me do. All you care about is that funky ass change. You and pops live in two different worlds, but both of you are the same. He loves the church more than me and you love these streets!" I said, shouting at her. "I found my wife. Someone you will never meet. You won't even see me walk down the aisle because you're too fucked up to realize that you're going to die out here," I finished.

She still hadn't looked at me and it only hurt more. I stuck my hand in my pocket, giving her a hundred-dollar bill. I slid my helmet on, looking at her one last time before riding off. I need to clear my head and the only person I could do that with right now was Pretty.

"I'm coming baby."

It had been a few days since being at the hospital. Grandma G was doing better. She had a heart attack but made it through. Since her stay was longer than expected, I wanted to make sure she got the care she needed to recover. I made sure she had the best of everything. The goal was to take some of the weight off Diamond. The nigga hasn't been right since it happened on his birthday. Sitting in the hospital with all of them watching the fear grasping them in a chokehold made me reflect.

It made me want to battle it. If fear was a person, I'd light his ass up twenty times over. The way it captured one's mind and body has you in some sort of chokehold you can't escape. I blared the music throughout my home to take my mind off

167

the situation. Lola had been blowing my phone up since I missed meeting up with her as promise. If she knew like I did Grandma G, going into the hospital saved her life.

I began thinking about Bookstore Girl. I'd almost wished she would have let me fuck her one good time before I dipped off. She was like a mystery; one I wasn't sure if I wanted to crack. The way we didn't know each other, but kept running into each other was the most exciting thing I had going on other than when I was on my bike.

I had my mind made up. I was leaving first thing tomorrow. Harvey and the guys would have to forgive me for not telling them, but this was my personal journey. I moved around puffing on my blunt when the sound of the doorbell went off. Niggas never rang my bell. I put the blunt out, blowing the smoke as I headed to the door. My head flew back because the only time I'd seen this person was in the hospital. "Does Diamond know?" she spat, brushing past me into my house.

"The fuck are you talking about and don't be walking in my shit like you pay a mortgage," I grumbled, closing the door behind her.

"He doesn't. Do any of your friends know?" she asked again.

I stood there, chin up. "They don't." She nodded.

I pinched the bridge of my nose. "Wait. Hold the fuck up. How did you know where I live?"

She held out a folder. "I checked. When I saw you the night Diamond's grandmother was admitted, I knew you looked familiar. The way your eyes sat off in the distance I knew you were scared. So, I asked Diamond your name. When he told me I checked."

I eased up to her, snatching the file out of her hand. "You're willing to get fired from your job to confront me about some shit that does not concern you?"

She leaned back on my couch. "When I saw how distraught Diamond was about his grandmother," she shook her head. "Then how close you all were. How you guys prayed together," She raised her eyes to me. "I'd wondered how he would feel if he knew one of his friends was—"

I swallowed deep. "Don't fucking say it!" I gritted.

The sound of the word made my stomach turn. It's what's been gripping me these last few months. I tried to ignore it, pushing it to the back of my mind, but every day there was a reminder of my fate. Anger surged through me as we stood there, glancing at each other. "How the fuck you know Diamond anyway. With yo nosy ass!" I snapped.

She lifted from the couch heading toward the door, "I deal with many people like you. Angry, hurt, and scared because instead of fighting you're giving up. Your attitude doesn't scare me. I met Diamond through Preach; he's dating my sister. I'm Rayana." She smiled. "I won't tell Diamond anything because it's not my place I—"

"Well fine time to realize your place"

She gave a tight lip smile. Before walking out. "I think you should fight, but it's obvious you've made up your mind. The least you can do is not be selfish and tell your friends the truth."

I slammed the door behind her. Karma played no games. She was coming around fast and taking me with her. I knew that me leaving tomorrow was the best thing. I rushed back to the room and started packing my shit. My friends would have to just forgive me because I was out of this bitch.

I sat Indian style in my living room, meditating. Focused on my Crown and Root Chakras, saying affirmations to myself. *I understand I need to move forward. I understand that my time here has ended. I am great at everything I do. I am that bitch.* I chanted.

I had been stuck on house arrest for the past week. Navi got me out, but I hadn't spoken to her since. I knew I messed up by doing what I did, but to know Cortez had money I had worked so hard for, I couldn't bear it. I hated that I even allowed him that type of power over me. I finished up my meditation by burning sage, cleaning out my space. I lit a small joint, puffing on it as I moved my body around my place, embracing the weed and the music. Honestly, I was struggling between not talking to my sisters, being stuck in the goddamn house, and wanting to feel free.

I picked my phone up off the table to call Navi. Apologizing was the first thing I was going to do when she answered. The phone rang a few times before going to voicemail. My sister was truly upset with me.

I thought about the mystery guy. If I would have gone home with him that night, I wouldn't be in this position to begin with. My pride. My fucking pride was too big sometimes. I believe it blocked what the universe had in store for me. The truth was, I was running from everything, including myself. I glanced back down at my phone so my mind wouldn't take a regretful trip. I scrolled through my emails and noticed someone had put in an offer for my bookstore. My eyes lit up at the offer. It wasn't worth as much as the person offered. I thought about rejecting it because I really wanted to keep my place, but I knew with a fancier place only blocks away from my business I didn't stand a chance. I took a deep breath and replied.

I was about to embark on a new journey. I wanted to explore and get the hell away from California, but first I needed to get off house arrest. I got up, pacing the floor, thinking of a way to get out of this. I could go to daddy and beg him to pull some strings, but we'd all promised we wouldn't share this with him. I only had to wear it for a month. *I could do a month.* I thought.

Then the idea of Cortez coming to get me popped in my head. I knew how evil he could be and there was no telling what he had planned since trying to rob his ass. "Nope!"

I hurried to my room and began packing. I was going to get this ankle monitor off and make a run for it. It didn't matter anyway because I'd fucked up the relationship with Navi and Rayana was so focused on her job; she didn't even call to check on me.

I knew what I was about to do would really put fire under Navi, because she had already risked a lot for me, but I had to. When the money came through from my store, I would send her a check enough to keep her straight for a while.

I was leaving, and I wasn't coming back.

I headed to pick up Pretty to take her out. She and I had been spending more time together. Although we hadn't been together long, I knew she was my person. Pretty made me feel like a king, something I'd never felt before. We loved each other and to others it may seem so sudden, but I was a sure man and sure about her.

Today was special for me. I was taking a leap of faith. I was going to ask Pretty to marry me. It was the perfect thing to do since I was preaching tomorrow. It felt like it was a step into the right direction. I still had my flaws, but I wanted to try. If she could make a sacrifice by stepping away from her job for me, I could do the same by taking care of her. I knew her father wouldn't approve, but frankly, I didn't give a damn.

THE STREETS & THE PULPIT

As I arrived at her house, I noticed her door was slightly open. I quickly got out of the car rushing to the door. *God, please don't make me have to send a nigga to the hot place cause they damn sure ain't coming up there.* I pushed the door open slowly, peeking inside. The house was dark but there were candles every fucking where. *Fuck going on in here?* Pretty crept out from the back fully naked, resting her hands on her waist.

"Damn, Pretty, you got it looking like you about to do a ritual in the muhfucka. I thought I was about to give somebody an expire date."

A light giggle fell from her lips. "Why are you like this?" she smiled. "I can protect myself you should know that by now. I'm still a person of the law."

"Yeah well, I'm still a person of Christ and the streets. Sometimes I can be hood and other times I can be holy. A holy hood nigga," I laughed.

I placed my gun on the table as I made my way up to her, wrapping my arms around her. "I was trying to take you out, but I see you have other plans."

She eased out of my grasp, strutting towards the back, "Yes, something like that." When she reached the room door, she held her hand out to stop me. "When you enter this room, I want everything from you. Don't hold back, please."

Pretty had passed the make love stage. She wanted to be fucked. I had given her what I thought she wanted. I gave her the gentle me, but if she wanted to be fucked, I was going to give her just that. I removed my shirt as I made my way toward her. When we entered the room, again candles every fucking where. My eyes bounced on everything in the room. *Handcuffs, whipped cream, ice, and beads.* "Are those ass beads?"

She laughed. "Their called anal—"

"I know what they are."

She nodded. She swayed her way to the bed sitting on a chest that sat at the foot of it. First, I grabbed the cuffs, "Hands out!" I barked.

"Preach I was thinking I—"

I tapped her nose. "You want to be fucked Pretty so let me do it, my way," I told her.

She slowly held both her hands out and I placed the cuffs on her wrists. I went to her drawer, opening it, looking for what I needed. "Why are you going through my stuff?"

"Shh," I whispered.

I saw something that caught my attention, but I ignored it for the moment. I grabbed a pair of thongs. I made my way back to the bed to stand her up. I made her stand on the chest with her cuffed hands in the air. I took the thong, tying it around the top of the bedpost, connecting the cuffs to it. "Now open your fucking legs and don't be shy," I instructed her.

Taking a piece of ice in my hand, I glided it across her pelvic up her stomach and around her nipples. "Sa-sa, oo," she moaned.

Trickles of the melted ice dripped down her stomach. My tongue captured every single drop. "Ooo," her body shook.

"Enjoy Pretty, I want to hear every moan, every cry, let go baby," I said as I moved the ice down to her pretty pussy. "I'm going to fuck you but first I want to play."

Whip cream. I shook the can while glaring at her. "Just. Enjoy. It."

I stuck the nozzle of the can into her pussy, releasing the cream inside her. "Oh, my fucking, shit!"

The cream trickled down, I sat on the chest with my head arched up sucking all of it out of her. The way my tongue explored her insides my shit was swimming. I could feel her clit thumping. I sucked on that muhfucka like I was trying to detach it. I felt her legs begin trembling. I stuck two fingers inside of her as I ate her pussy. "Prentice, ah, baby arrrgghh," she growled.

Her body bounced slightly, trying to keep up with my tongue and fingers. When I removed my fingers from her, I slid them back and forth, circling her asshole. I was about to take Pretty to a different place somewhere she had never been and will never want to leave. *Anal Beads.* I released her from the bedpost but kept her hands cuffed. I gently laid her on her back. Taking the thong, I tied one of her ankles to one end and went to grab another pair, tying her other leg to the other end. Pretty was spread wide as hell. I came out of my clothes. I stroked my dick a few times before approaching her.

"Now I'm going to fuck you."

She was nice and wet, sticky and that pussy was thumping something crazy. I climbed on top of her, kissing her nastily. Our tongues explored each other as I entered her. Pretty moaned in my mouth.

Roll up, then down. Side to side.

Her eyes sat low as she took her bottom lip into her mouth. "Do you love me?" I asked.

She nodded.

"Say it!"

"I love *you! Ah!*"

I stuck the anal beads inside her all the way to the third ball. I used one hand, pushing her arms above her head to hold them down while the other gripped her waist.

Roll up, then down. Side to side.

"You mean everything to me Pretty," I moaned.

Roll up, then down. Side to side.

"Me too," she muttered.

Roll up, then down. Side to side.

178

"Pretty, I love you."

Roll up, then down. Side to side.

I watched her face as she enjoyed everything I was giving her. The more I gazed into her eyes, the more I knew she was the one. She didn't have to worry about another woman. She would never go hungry; she would never have to use a dime of her money. Hell, if I could carry her anywhere, she wanted to go, I would. I was that invested, but there was problem.

Roll up, then down. Side to side.

"Pretty you still working the case?"

"Wha-what?"

I removed my hand from her wrist, taking the other side of her hip into my hand. Now the rolls became pounds to her pussy. I was digging her out so much, her titties were slapping her in the face. "Are you working the case still."

"Uh, ah no-no-no!" she screamed loudly. "I'm cumin Prentice."

My gut told me she was lying, but I wanted to trust her. I dropped my head as I finished up. "Oh shit!" I howled.

Pretty and I had cum together. With the heat from the candles and the heavy panting we were doing, I needed some air. I released her from everything and headed into the bathroom to shower. Something just didn't feel right. I saw the case file in her drawer and if she was off the case, as she said, why was it there? I ran the shower, but before getting in, I just need to say a quick prayer.

God, please give me a sign if marrying her is the right decision.

Preach headed to the shower as I began cleaning up the room. The way this man just did my body, I couldn't walk away if I wanted to. Preach had become a necessary part of my life. I couldn't lose him. I didn't want to. I really needed to talk to him about the situation with Zaria. I was so mad at her because she didn't know what situation she put me.

They gave her house arrest, and it was only to make sure she didn't go near Cortez for a while. It was a decision of helping my sister or giving up Chevy. I still haven't had a real chance to get to him like I wanted to. I saw him at the party, but it was only for a second. The man was like a king. They all looked up to him. The way he worked the room was something I'd never seen before. Unfortunately, I was back on the case, but I was not the lead detective. The person they put in my place was someone who would stop at nothing to be on the top.

I had been trying to stall on the little piece of information I had. However, someone, I believe my daddy, had his hands in it, even from home. I knew I needed to tell Preach, but with the love that poured out of him it was hard. Even with him asking me, I couldn't. I figured I could think of a way to get them off Chevy's ass. I just needed more time.

I heard the shower turn off and my eyes landed right on the bathroom door. When he exited the bathroom, he glanced at me. Normally, anytime he looked at me, he smiled, but something seemed off. My stomach curled into a knot.

I was thinking of ways to explain this without him getting upset. I did it for my sister, my blood as he would do for Zoo, I'm sure. He put his clothes on as he talked to me, "I want to see you in church tomorrow, Navi," he said.

Navi? He hadn't called me that since the day I officially met him. Something was up. "What's wrong?" I asked.

Preach side-eyed me. "Nothing, I'm just thinking about tomorrow." He had now put his shirt on. "God is giving me a message and I need to put it all together. No more sex until we're married," he said as he headed out of the bedroom.

I rushed behind him. "What? Wait. No more sex, how long am I supposed to wait?"

"If you love me like you say you do. Waiting shouldn't be a problem. Remember, I'm still a man of God and he just told me he who finds a wife finds a good thing, and obtains favor from the Lord. So again," this time he turned toward me. "If you're a good thing, waiting shouldn't be a problem and me putting a ring on your finger shouldn't be long. I will see you at church tomorrow, Navi," he finished, kissing me on the cheek then leaving.

I stood there with so many thoughts going through my head. The way Preach just flipped into a different person before my eyes; I didn't know what to think. I knew he wasn't a stupid man. Either he found out that I was working on the case, and that's why he asked, or he was genuinely ready to embrace his calling and wanted to approach it correctly. Nevertheless, I had to choose between moving forward with my job or resigning, as I couldn't stay in the same field while knowing what Preach did and still maintain my integrity.

I tightened the strap on my robe, took a deep breath and got on my knees. Preach always talk about praying. I was going to pray and hope that God was listening.

I had been up all-night picking at the ankle monitor, trying to get it off. Everything I had tried didn't work, and I was becoming frustrated. "Ugh!" I screamed as I laid back on the bed. I was wasting so much time on this, and I could have been miles away by now. I sat up in my bed, trying to think. "What the hell can I use," I said aloud.

I got up from the bed walking into the bathroom. I grabbed the scissors. I didn't intend to destroy it, only to open it and remove the attached piece. I played with it for a while and boom; the shit slid right out. I left the monitor on the bed, grabbed my bag and a small sweater. I took one last look at my place before leaving out and never to looking back. I didn't want to take my car, so I walked up the street to the bus stop.

THE STREETS & THE PULPIT

While I waited, I turned my location off on my phone, reset it and threw it in the nearby trash. Once the bus came, I got on, taking a deep breath. I was going to the Greyhound station.

As the bus passed the city by, I reminiscenced on the good parts of California that I would miss. The bus stopped a block from my store. Although I should have stayed on the bus, I wanted to see my place one last time before it was off to the new owner. I grabbed my bag before getting off the bus. I strolled up the street until I reached the front of it. Tears filled my eyes. *You need to spice shit up in here. Add plants, a little orange color to make it pop.* The sound of the mystery man popped in my head. I giggled to myself.

I had envisioned something spectacular for this place. It was supposed to be the perfect spot for someone to enjoy a healthy treat and read a good ass book by black authors. It was supposed to be a place of peace and solace. This place was supposed to be my freedom, but somehow had become a burden. It was a bittersweet goodbye to a dream that I had since I was a little girl, opening her first book, getting lost in the story.

I stepped back to take one last look at the tiny juice bar I had created, when I felt a pair of hands over my mouth and waist. I was being drug backwards, scarping the backs of my heels on the concrete. I tried tussling to get away, but whoever it was wouldn't let up. I felt my body being tossed onto cold steel as the impact from the throw knocked the wind out of me. The sounds of men chuckling filled my ears. When I looked up, they all had a mask on. "Who are you?" I mumbled.

Neither of them said a word as the van I was in sped down the streets. My eyes bounced all over the back of the van to the back door. I quickly crawled toward the doors to open it and jump out but felt my head being snatched back. The sound of my hair ripping from my scalp was so potent. When he pulled me back, I noticed a tattoo. It was the same one from the guys that had come looking for Cortez. Blaze N Fire. They had lost the race, so I didn't know why they were coming after me.

I sat in the corner with my knees to my chest, shaking. I needed to get out of this van before they killed me. It was now or never. I struck, punching at the guy in front of me, throwing blows. Another guy shoved me so hard my head hit the metal frame and before I knew it, everything went black.

Sleep hadn't been easy for me these last few months, and last night wasn't an exception. I meditated some, smoked some, and even paced the floor. I tried to convince myself to stay a little while longer. I wanted to give Harvey the time I'd promised. However, the more I thought about Rayana popping up and Lola confronting me, the more staying longer became nonexistent.

I got up from the bed preparing for a long road trip. I packed up my car, locked up my house, leaving a yellow envelope for Harvey. She never knocked. She knew where to go to get the key, so I knew she would see what I'd left. I took one last look at my house before getting in the Caprice and taking off down the road.

THE STREETS & THE PULPIT

As I drove on the highway, I received a text message from Preach asking me to come to church. I didn't bother to open it fully so he wouldn't know I'd read the message. Preach was a special kid. Although he was a part of the Zoo, I knew his calling was really in the church. The nigga didn't smoke, barely put a drink to his lips and only used a gun when he needed to. He was probably the reason none of us had gotten caught, because he stayed prayed up.

Unfortunately, he had parents whose minds were on everything else but their own son. I played with the thought of stepping foot in the church, but struggled with it. God had only offered me loyal friends and nothing more. I felt he had cursed me. Why did he choose me to be in this position? I didn't know. Did I want to talk to him to tell him all my problems, my worries, no. I just wanted him to allow me the time to see my mother. It was all I'd asked for.

I took the first exit on the main street. I passed by my business, which was only a few blocks from Bookstore Girl. I was hoping to see her so that I could tell her I had purchased her place, and she could keep it and the money. I wanted to invest in her business because I could see the potential and the love she had put into it. As I turned on to the street a van damn near hit me, swerving over and continuing straight. I should have shot the tires off that muhfucka, but decided against it.

THE STREETS & THE PULPIT

When I pulled up in front of the store, it was still closed, as if she hadn't been by in days. I quickly got out, sliding an envelope underneath the door. I would know if she got it because she would call. I jogged back to my car and sped off. The last stop I made was the church. I sat in my car watching as everyone went in. I debated on it. I sat in the car a good ten minutes fighting with myself. It was now or never.

What really compelled me to get out is when I saw his mother staggering up to the church. If she could be there for her son, I could be here to support my brother. I got out of the car and walked toward the door. With each step I took, my feet felt like they were getting heavier by the second. My gut was telling me to turn around, get in the Caprice and take the fuck off like I planned. However, the sound of Preach's voice seeped through the door when his mom opened it.

He's preaching? I walked inside, through the small hall, and stood in the doorway. My nigga was in the pulpit giving a sermon.

I felt like a proud father while he was in his element.

I sat in the back-room room reading through my bible. Repeating the same line over and over. "Pride, Pray and acceptance is something God can provide." I mumbled.

Since leaving Pretty's, I hadn't had a wink of sleep. Between me going back and forth with God of what I should say and practicing what my father would want me to say was an all-night battle. I invited all my friends to church today because I was hoping the message I would deliver was one that could touch all of them. I'd texted Chevy separately, asking him to come, but he hadn't even read the message.

A tap on the door sent my head shooting up. "The choir is almost done," an usher said to me.

THE STREETS & THE PULPIT

I nodded as I stood from my father's desk. I clutched the bible in my hand as I walked out of the room. I wanted to keep the tradition, so I wore my father's pulpit robe. The black thick robe fit almost perfectly. I walked down the hall to the soft keys of the piano and base of the drums. I blew out a deep breath. The usher glanced at me and smiled. "Let God use you."

I stepped out onto the pulpit. I glanced out into the church, and it was a full house. I spotted Harvey, Zu, and Foe. They all sat together. A row in front of them was Diamond. Although Grandma G was still in the hospital, Diamond still came. I could see him snickering like a kid. My eyes then landed on Navi and one of her sisters, her mother and father.

My father walked up to me, leaning in, "You got this son."

I stepped up to the podium, opening my bible as some clapped their hands and others bobbed their heads to the music. I nervously closed my eyes. *Let God use you.* I shook the nerves and started, "Praise the Lord saints," I called out. "I said, Praise the lord saints!"

"Praise the Lord," some of them called out.

My nerves were getting the best of me. "Preach brother!" an older lady shouted.

"Let him use you!" someone else said.

I smiled. "Can I be honest this Sunday? I had something prepared for y'all, but I think I want to do it the way God is telling me to." I paused. "I'm a man of honesty, loyalty," I looked at Navi, then my boys. "I'm not perfect, but the thing that pushes me to try to be better not just for myself, but for God is pride, prayer and acceptance." I pointed into the crowd. "I don't know if what I'm about to say can help somebody, but I hope so. I want you to walk out of here knowing you can be redeemed. That God has a place for you and it's never too late to get right with him."

Some people nodded. Some people stared.

"We all have a past, we all have the demon chasing us, but *God!*" I shouted. "But God—"

The sight of my mother walking into the church made my body still. I glanced at my father, who saw her too. He looked back at me and nodded. *Keep going.* He mouthed.

A lady stood up and shouted. "Preach, preacher!"

That's when I spotted Chevy. He stood in the doorway, hesitating to walk in. The usher stepped to him, guiding him to the pew. He sat in the far back alongside my mother. I nodded and smiled. I felt a rush go through, as if a spirit had taken over.

"First Peter chapter five verse seven. Cast all your anxiety on him because he cares for you. That fear of the unknown is normal, but you must trust that God can order your steps. He can save you. He can heal you. He can give you a love that you never felt!" I picked up the mic. "The anger in your heart, get it out. That pride that's blocking you put it to the side. Fear, it doesn't exist because you're giving it to God. Trust that he will see you through. Sinners have souls too. I'm not saying to go out and commit a crime and it's okay. What I am saying is God knows we're not perfect, but we cannot let our pride get in the way of prayer, Amen? We must accept that we are all sinners trying to get to the same place, heaven!"

I watched while everyone sat in silence, gazing at me. I cleared my throat and continued. "Let me repeat that for those in the back," I said, pacing behind the podium. "I said," I paused, looking at Chevy and my mother. "We have to accept that we are all sinners trying to get to the same place."

Diamond stood up clapping, "Betta Preach!"

I saw the usher throw her hands up. "Yes, yes God!"

"*Pride!*" I yelled

The piano keys started up again.

"Well!" Diamond yelled.

"*Prayer!*"

The drums rolled in.

"*Oh lawd!*" Diamond hummed.

"Acceptance is all we want. We can get that with just prayer and forgiveness, so give it, give it all to God."

I finished, looking to my father, who sat there with a smile on his face. He was proud. I'd finally made him proud. My mother had walked up to the altar holding her arms out to me. I didn't care she had just come off the street into the church or that she had probably gotten high before walking in here. I reached out to her, hugging her tightly. "I'm proud of you, son," she mumbled.

Tears tickled out of my eyes. "I love you ma," I cried.

"I love you too."

"*Glory!*" The Deacon shouted as they went into praise dancing. Stomping and shouting.

My eyes landed Navi, who held a smile on her face as she came up to me. She reached out, pulling me in for a hug. "I love you Prentice, I'm proud of you," she whispered.

I held her tightly as my eyes landed on Chevy, who went to exit the church. He turned to look at me. *Proud of you, my nigga.* He mouthed.

As he went to turn to leave, two men approached him in suits. They pulled out a pair of cuffs and my eyes quickly bounced on Navi, "What did you do?" I gritted.

She held a confused stare as she turned to look at Chevy, then back at me, "I swear it was not me Preach, I swear," her eyes watered.

Her father stepped in front of me with a sinister smile on his face. Navi pulled his arm back. "What did you do!" she screamed, causing everyone to look at us.

He leaned in to the both of us. "What I had to."

THE STREETS & THE PULPIT

My eyes landed back on Chevy, who hadn't even turned my way. I glanced at my brothers and Harvey, who looked just as sick as I did as the detectives walked Chevy out of the church in cuffs.

This was not what I prayed for.

.

THE STREETS & THE PULPIT

LETTER TO MY READERS

If you have made it to the end of this, let me say how much I appreciate you. I hoped you enjoyed the story as much as I enjoyed writing it. The story continues. What will happen between Preach and Navi?

Grandma G will she fully recover, or will she leave Diamond with a broken heart because we all know he doesn't play about his granny?

Foe, Harvey and Zu; Are you still curious? What happened in the room between Foe and Harvey? Do you believe him, or do you think more happened?

Chevy no matter how hard he tries to move forward; he seems to get pushed back. Do you think the Zoo will save Bookstore girl or will Navi have to pull some strings?

There is so much more to happen with the Zoo. As you know, I won't tell you who's next, but it's coming.

Tiktok: Fresheebabii
IG: Freshiebabii/authortatiana

Til the next one, fairies!